* * * * * * *

It was already dark when the bus stopped with a jerk at the bus stop on the corner. Chester had been lying on the floor at his master's feet. He instinctively knew that it was the bus stop where they were to get off. He stood up and gently put his nose down on Kandace's knee to let her know that he was ready to lead her home.

"Good boy," she said as she reached down and patted him lovingly on the head.

Kandace put the shoulder strap of her purse over her shoulder and picked up her briefcase from the floor beside her. Taking hold of Chester's harness with her free hand, she stood up and carefully worked her way to the door of the bus. The bus driver patiently waited as Kandace found her way down the steps and off the bus onto the sidewalk.

* * * * * * *

Other titles by J.E. Terrall available in

LARGE PRINT EDITION

Western Short Stories
    The Old West
    The Frontier
    Untamed Land
    Tales from the Territory
    Frontier Justice

Western Novels
    Conflict in Elkhorn Valley
    The Story of Joshua Higgins
    The Valley Ranch War

Romance Novels
    Sing for Me
    Return to Me
    Forever Yours

Mystery/Suspense/Thriller
    I Can See Clearly
    The Return Home
    Murder in the Backcountry

I CAN SEE CLEARLY

by

J. E. Terrall

ISBN: 978-0-999782-1-6

This is a work of fiction. Names, characters, and incidents are either a product of the author's imagination or are used fictitiously, and any resemblance to actual persons, living or dead, is purely coincidental.

Printed in the United States of America
First Printing / 2014 – www.lulu.com
Second Printing / 2014 - www.creatspace.com
Third Printing / 2018 - www,creatspace.com
    Larger Print Edition
Cover: Front cover by Phyllis Terrall

Book Layout /
Formatting: J.E. Terrall
                Custer, South Dakota

I CAN SEE CLEARLY

To my Daughter, Susan

PROLOGUE

To look at Kandace Clarke, one would never know that she was blind. She stood tall and straight and carried herself well. Many a man had looked at her and admired her figure as well as the smoothness of her complexion and the soft shine of her shoulder length hair. There was no doubt in anyone's mind that Kandace was an exceptionally good looking woman, and an exceptional woman given her blindness.

Kandace walked briskly along the sidewalk. In one hand she held a leather briefcase while in the other she gripped the stiff leather handle of the harness on her large German Shepherd, Chester. Chester walked along the sidewalk with the same confidence in his job that his master showed in hers.

Chester had been her Seeing Eye dog for more than four years. Kandace had grown to depend on Chester to help her get around. Chester was not only her eyes; he was her constant companion, friend, protector, and her independence.

Since her move to Fort Collins, Colorado, just two years before, they would walk the three blocks to the bus stop, then the two blocks to the office where Kandace worked. At the end of the day, they would return to her apartment by the same route.

As they would approach each corner, Chester would slow and then step in front of his master to make sure that she stopped before stepping off the curb out into the street. Kandace would reach down and pat the dog on the neck. As soon as traffic had stopped and the street was clear, Chester would move to her side and step down off the curb. That was her signal that Chester was ready to move on.

As soon as she stepped down next to him, he would guide her safely across the street. He would stop her at the other side until she stepped back up onto the sidewalk again then would lead her on. This was the normal routine for both of them. The two of them moved as one, except today.

CHAPTER ONE

The wind was brisk and cold, and the air was damp. It seemed that winter would soon be returning after several days of unusually warm weather. There were already a few flurries in the air. If the weather reports were correct, it would not be long before the streets of Fort Collins, Colorado, would be covered with a thick blanket of fresh new snow.

It was already dark when the bus stopped with a jerk at the bus stop on the corner. Chester had been lying on the floor at his master's feet. He instinctively knew that it was the bus stop where they were to get off. He stood up and gently put his nose down on Kandace's knee to let her know that he was ready to lead her home.

"Good boy," she said as she reached down and patted him lovingly on the head.

Kandace put the shoulder strap of her purse over her shoulder and picked up her briefcase from the floor beside her. Taking hold of Chester's harness with her free hand, she stood up and carefully worked her way to the door of the bus. The bus driver patiently waited as Kandace found her way down the steps and off the bus onto the sidewalk.

"See you Monday, Miss Clarke. You, too, Chester," the bus driver said.

"Thank you, Frank. See you Monday," Kandace replied.

Once on the sidewalk, it took just a moment for Kandace to get her bearings before she motioned for Chester to lead the way. The big dog knew what he was supposed to do. He had been doing it almost every day for the past two years. He stepped across in front of his master, gently forcing her to turn in the direction they needed to go. As soon as he was sure that she was ready, they began the three-block walk home.

They covered the first block with ease and were on their way along the second block when Kandace began to feel a slight hesitation in Chester's movements. It seemed to her that he was suddenly reluctant to keep going, almost as if he were confused or lost. She knew they still had at least two more streets to cross, but there must be something up ahead that troubled the big dog.

"What is it, Chester?" she asked as if she expected him to speak to her and tell her what it was that he could see that she could not.

Suddenly, Chester turned and stepped in front of her, forcing her to stop. Kandace was surprised by his strange behavior. He had never stopped her in the middle of the block like this before, but he must have seen something or heard something.

Maybe there was an alley in the middle of the block and something was in the alley that made Chester cautious. She wished that he could talk to her and tell her what was going on.

She stood quietly and listened very carefully in an effort to hear even the slightest sound that might give her a clue as to Chester's strange behavior, but she could not hear anything unusual. There were the usual sounds that are typical of the streets in many cities; an occasional car going by, distant music from an apartment and the sound of the breeze blowing between the buildings.

Her sensitive hearing picked up another sound she had not heard for a very long time. It was the sound of the deep, almost inaudible growl that came from deep inside Chester's broad chest. She had only heard him growl like that once before when another large dog had threatened Kandace's safety several years ago.

Kandace did not know just what to do or which way to turn. If there was another dog near by, she could not hear it. She could feel Chester pushing against her legs as he slowly backed up, gently but firmly forcing her to take a step backward. The uncertainty of what was happening was beginning to frighten her and she gripped Chester's harness tighter.

Suddenly, she realized that whatever was causing Chester to act so strangely, holding onto his harness so tightly would prevent him from protecting her. Yet, she did not want to let him loose. Reluctantly, but very carefully, she reached down to the collar around Chester's neck and unsnapped his leash. She kept a light hold of his harness so that he could be free to move if need be; yet still guide her away from danger if he could.

"Well, looky what's we got here."

The sudden sound of a male voice startled Kandace, causing her to take another step backward. The tone in the man's voice struck fear in her heart. The man's words sounded a little slurred as if the man might be drunk, or at least had been drinking.

"Hey, man, knock it off. You scarin' the little lady. We don't want to scare her none, now, do we?"

The voice of the second man was deeper and smoother, yet just as frightening to her. His words did little to help ease Kandace's fears. It was the first time she had encountered anyone that Chester immediately responded to in such a defensive manner. It was clear by Chester's reaction that he considered them a threat to his master's safety.

Kandace could feel the tension in Chester's body through his harness, and sensed the danger that Chester felt.

"Please, let me pass," Kandace said as firmly as possible. Kandace knew that her voice sounded weak, but she could not help it. The cold chill that consumed her was not caused by the cold winter breeze, but from the sheer terror that she was feeling.

"Lady, you better call off that dog 'for we have to hurt him bad."

"Easy Chester," she said softly in an effort to get him to at least stop growling.

Chester obeyed her instantly as he pushed back against her leg. However, he stood in front of her and never took his eyes off the two men. He continued to stay ready to defend his master at the slightest hint of movement toward her by these men.

"Why don't you just hand over that there purse of yours," the man with the deeper voice said. "No need of anybody gettin' hurt."

"And that there briefcase, too," the other man added sharply.

"Yeah, the briefcase, too."

Although the man with the deeper voice did not have the threatening quality in his voice that the other man had, he still had the tone of a strong demand and his meaning was clear. He said it as if it were just a simple request, yet the threat of bodily harm for failure to comply was definitely there.

"Come on, man. Take the damn purse. She can't see us noways," the man who had been drinking said impatiently as he stepped toward Kandace.

The man's sudden movement toward Kandace, along with the urgency and harshness of his demand, caused Chester to take immediate action. He lunged at the man, pulling himself free of Kandace's loose grip on his harness. In one swift bound, Chester leaped up and grabbed the man by the arm, quickly knocking him to the ground. The man screamed in pain as Chester's sharp teeth quickly penetrated the man's jacket sleeve and cut deep into his arm.

"Chester!" Kandace screamed as she lost her balance and fell to the ground on her hands and knees.

She could hear Chester growling and the two men yelling and screaming. One was cursing the dog, while the other was screaming in pain.

Suddenly, she heard Chester cry out in pain as she heard what only could be someone kicking him, or hitting him with something very hard. Her heart almost stopped and panic gripped her as her fear for Chester's safety consumed her.

"Chester!" she cried out again as she knelt on the ground and flung her arms around wildly as she tried to find Chester in her darkness.

Suddenly, she felt someone grab her purse. As the man pulled on the purse, Kandace was knocked over. In her struggle with her attacker, she held onto the shoulder strap of the purse in kind of a tug-of-war. Finally, the shoulder strap broke against the tugging and jerking on it, causing her to fall over backward. It caused her to hit the back of her head on the hard sidewalk. The impact dazed her slightly and caused her to lose her sense of direction. Managing to get up on her hands and knees, she began crawling around on the sidewalk in an effort to find Chester, but she could not find him.

"Chester!" she called out as she stopped and listened in her effort to find him, but there was no sound to help her locate him, only the sound of a man laughing and another cursing in pain.

"Kill that damn mutt"

It was the voice of the first man, the one that Chester had attacked. Her stomach wrenched as her life without Chester flashed through her mind, and her eyes filled with tears.

"Oh, God. Please don't hurt him any more. Please," she begged.

As Kandace pleaded with her attackers, she reached out and felt a pant leg only inches from her face. She grabbed the man's pant leg and pulled on it.

"Please, please don't hurt my dog any more. Take the purse, but don't hurt him, please" she pleaded as the man tried to pull himself free of her grip on his leg.

"We already gots the purse, lady," the man with the deeper voice said. "Now, let go, damn you."

She refused to let go of him as he tried to jerk free from her. Her grip was strong and he could not pull himself free. He wrapped the shoulder strap of her purse around his hand, then swung her purse over his head bringing it down hard along side Kandace's head. The sudden impact of the heavy purse on the side of her head made her let go.

She felt the blow, but only for a split second. There was a brief sensation of pain and bright flashing lights like stars before her eyes, then nothing. Everything had gone silent and blank.

* * * *

"Miss, Miss."

Kandace could hear a voice that seemed to be calling her from off in the distance. It sounded rather faint at first, but seemed to be getting closer with each word. There was also the sensation of floating, of spinning around and around without touching anything. As the sensation began to fade, the feeling of pain on the side of her head began to take its place.

Suddenly, she realized that someone was holding on to her and the earlier events quickly returned through the fog in her mind. Unable to see who was there, she started throwing her arms around in an effort to fight off who she believed to be her attackers.

"Whoa, Lady! Settle down. I'm not going to hurt you."

The sound of the man's voice sank into her consciousness and registered as being different from the voices she had heard before everything went blank. She stopped whirling her arms around and settled down long enough to listen.

"You're going to be all right. There's an ambulance on the way."

The voice she heard was pleasant with an almost soothing quality to it. It was nothing like the harsh voices of the other two men. His voice seemed to have a calming effect on her already frayed nerves. It was the voice of someone who seemed to care about her and wanted to help her. She raised her hands and was about to touch him when she remembered Chester.

"Chester! Oh, my God. Where is Chester?" she asked as panic began to grip her again. She tried to free herself from the man's arms, but he would not let go of her.

"Who's Chester?" the man asked as he held her and tried to calm her so that she would not hurt herself any more.

"My dog," she replied with a deep pang of despair.

"He's lying over by the building. I'm sorry, lady. He's hurt pretty bad."

"Please, help me. Help me to him."

Her eyes were filled with tears and her voice choked slightly at her request. She turned away from the man holding her and reached out in an effort to find her dog, but she could not find him.

Jason Barrett could see the pain in her eyes and the tears roll down her cheeks. His heart went out to her. He took her hand and gently placed it on the dog's head.

"He's here, Miss," he said softly.

"Oh, God," she said as she jerked her hand back fearing that Chester was already dead.

As she turned away from the dog, she found herself back in the man's arms. Tears streaked down her cheeks as she cried openly, no longer able to control her emotions. Wrapping her arms around the man's neck, she buried her face in his shoulder and hung on to him as she wept. After a moment or two, she raised her head from the man's shoulder and looked up at him.

"Is, - - is he dead?"

It was difficult for her to get the words out.

"No, he's not dead, but he's hurt pretty bad."

"Can you help him, please?"

"I'll try. What's your name?"

"Kandace Clarke."

"I'm Jason Barrett. Are you all right?"

"Yes, I think so."

"I've called for an ambulance. It will be here soon. Just relax and everything will be fine."

Kandace thought she could hear what sounded like people milling around. She could also hear the faint sound of sirens off in the distance that seemed to be rapidly coming closer.

"Here's the ambulance," a voice from the crowd said as someone came up close to her.

"Thanks, officer."

"How's she doing, Lieutenant?"

"I don't know, but she seems to be doing okay right now. Call the animal control officer and have him come pick up the dog."

Every muscle in Kandace's body suddenly tightened at the words "animal control officer". To her that meant that Chester would be taken to the dog pound and put to sleep.

"No, please don't let them take him away," Kandace pleaded.

"It's all right," Jason reassured her. "I'll see to it that your dog is taken care of, you just relax. I'm not going to let them put him to sleep. They will take him to an animal shelter where he will be well cared for."

Kandace hesitated for a second, then slowly settled back in Jason's arms. It had never been easy for her to trust others, but for some reason that she didn't understand she trusted him. She didn't understand why she felt the way she did about him, but she felt safe and secure leaning against him.

She closed her eyes as the pain from the side of her head gradually turned into a splitting headache. She could also feel the pain in her hands and knees from falling to the pavement.

Suddenly, she heard the sound of a vehicle stopping just a few feet away. It sounded like several people rushing toward her.

"My name is Jennie. I'm a nurse and we are going to help you. How are you feeling?"

Kandace felt the warmth of a hand on her wrist. She quickly realized that the woman was taking her pulse.

"I have a headache, and my hands and knees hurt from falling."

"We'll help you," Jennie said as she glanced up at Jason.

Jennie quickly checked out the wounds on Kandace's hands and knees and found them to be only minor scratches requiring just cleaning and bandaging. Once again, Jennie glanced up at Jason and wondered who the handsome man was as she smiled at him.

Jason felt the need to explain why he was there. "I'm Lieutenant Barrett with the police department. I found her here on the sidewalk. She's been hit in the head with something that was fairly heavy. She's blind, but not from the hit on the head."

"I think I was hit with my purse before two men ran off with it. Is my briefcase around?"

"No," Jason replied after a quick look around. "They must have taken that, too."

Kandace flinched when Jennie reached up and pushed back her hair to examine the cut on the side of Kandace's head. It wasn't a very deep cut, but it did require cleaning and possibly a couple of stitches.

"You have a nasty cut on your head. We're going to take you to the hospital to get the cut taken care of, along with the cuts on your hands and knees," Jennie explained.

"I can't go until I'm sure Chester is taken care of," she protested.

Panic began to grip Kandace again as she thought of her dog and what might happen to him if she was not there to help him. She could not let anything happen to Chester, he was a big part of her life. She tried to pull herself away from Jason, but he held onto her.

"Relax, please. I promised that I would see to it that Chester is properly taken care of, and I will," Jason reassured her.

"But I can't just leave him."

"You go in the ambulance with the nurse. I will catch up with you at the hospital as soon as I am sure that Chester is in the hands of a good veterinarian, okay?"

"Okay," Kandace conceded reluctantly, knowing that she had little choice in the matter.

Jason helped Kandace sit up, then stepped back out of the way as the medical team from the ambulance lifted her up and put her on the stretcher. He watched as she was covered with a blanket and placed in the ambulance. Soon, the ambulance was speeding off down the street and around the corner out of sight.

Jason turned around and looked at the dog lying limp against the wall of the building. After a quick look around to see that the other officers on the scene were questioning people in the area in the hope of finding a witness or two, he walked over to the dog and knelt down beside it.

The dog was awake, but was having difficulty breathing. Jason was sure that the dog had some broken ribs and probably some internal injuries. He reached out and lightly touched the dog on the head, gently stroking his soft coat. Chester tried to raise his head and look at Jason, but couldn't seem to move very much.

"Easy does it, big guy. Help will be here in a minute," Jason said softly, trying to reassure the animal that he would be okay.

Within a few minutes, the animal control officer arrived. He took one look at Chester and shook his head.

"I don't think he has much of a chance."

"I want this dog taken to a veterinarian. I don't care what it costs. I want everything done that can be done to save this animal. Do you understand that?"

The tone of Jason's voice made his words sound like an order because that was just what it was, an order. The animal control officer looked at Jason as if he were asking for the world.

"He's probably not going to make it."

"You listen, and listen carefully. I'm Lieutenant Barrett. You get this dog to a good veterinarian and you do it now. Did you understand what I just told you?"

"Yes, sir."

"Then do it."

"Yes, sir. I'll get him to the best veterinarian in the city."

"As soon as you get him to a veterinarian, you call me at the Poudre Valley Hospital and let me know how the dog's doing."

"Yes sir."

Jason helped the animal control officer carefully pick up Chester and gently place him in the back of the truck. In seconds, the truck was on its way to a veterinarian.

Jason turned back and helped the other officers finish up their on-site investigation. When everything that could be done at the scene was completed, Jason returned to his car and drove directly to Poudre Valley Hospital.

CHAPTER TWO

Jason arrived at the hospital shortly before eight. Parking his car in the space reserved for official vehicles, he shut off the engine and pulled down the sun visor before getting out of the car. On the back of the sun visor was an official looking sticker that read "Fort Collins Police Department - Official Business".

Jason walked up the ramp and entered the hospital through the emergency entrance. He had been in the hospital many times and knew that the Admitting Desk was just up the hall. As he approached the Admitting Desk, he saw a woman talking to a young man. She appeared to be giving the man directions.

The woman glanced over at Jason as he walked toward her, but continued talking to the man. Jason stopped and watched while he waited for the woman to finish. As soon as the man left, the woman turned toward Jason and smiled. He stepped up to the desk.

"My name's Diana, can I help you?" she asked in a soft, pleasant voice.

"I hope so. I'm Lieutenant Barrett with the police department," he said as he held out his ID and badge for her to inspect.

"Well, I won't hold that against you," she said playfully.

"Well, I thank you for that," he said with a slight grin. "I'm looking for a woman who was brought in a little while ago after being attacked near Old Town. Her name is Clarke, Kandace Clarke. Can you tell me how she is doing and if I might be able to talk with her?"

"Oh, yes," Diana replied. "The doctor has just finished examining her. She is being admitted for observation."

"When would I be able to talk with her?"

"She's still in emergency room three. We haven't taken her to her room, yet. Let me see if she is up to having visitors."

"Thank you."

Jason leaned against the wall next to the desk while he watched Diana walk down the hall and disappear through a door. He was pretty sure that Ms. Clarke's first concern would be for her dog and he wondered what he was going to say to her. From the way she had reacted, the dog was more than a Seeing Eye dog to her.

He was reluctant to tell her what the animal control officer had told him, that the dog was not likely to live. He could see no reason to worry her more than she was already, especially with her injuries. But on the other hand, it might be best to be honest with her and prepare her for the worst.

So far, he had not received a report on the condition of her dog.

The closing of a door down the hall interrupted Jason's thoughts. He looked up and saw Diana coming toward him.

"Give her a couple of minutes, then you can go see her. She's in the second room on the left."

"Thank you," he replied as he turned and looked down the hall.

Jason looked at his watch and stared at the second hand as it slowly moved around the face of it. It seemed to move so slowly that it made him wonder if the battery in his watch was losing power.

"You can go in now," Diana said smiling at him from behind the desk.

Jason glanced over at her, nodded a thank you, then started down the hall. As he walked toward the room, he wondered if Kandace Clarke was a Miss or a Mrs. When he got to the door, he hesitated for a second, then knocked lightly on the door. A soft, pleasant voice told him to enter. Slowly, he pushed the door open and peered around it.

"Hi, how are you doing?" he asked not knowing just what to say and almost stumbling over his own words.

"Is that you Mr. Barrett? I'm sorry, Lieutenant Barrett."

"Yes, but please call me Jason."

"All right. I'm doing fine, Jason. I guess that they are going to admit me overnight for observation."

"Yes, I guess so. I'm sure that's a good idea. There's no sense taking any unnecessary risks. Is there anything I can do or get for you?"

"No, but thank you for asking. How is Chester? Will he be all right?" The tone of her voice and the slight glitch in it made it clear that she was very concerned about him.

"I still haven't heard anything. I told the animal control officer to take him to the best veterinarian in town. I'm sorry, but his juries are quite bad. I'm sure that he will get the best treatment possible."

"I'm sure. Would you be so kind as to let me know how he is doing as soon as you hear anything?"

"Of course."

She took a deep breath and let out a long sigh.

"I suppose you need to ask me a lot of questions."

"I need to know as much about the men who attacked you as you can remember."

"It's difficult with all that has happened. Let me think for a moment, please."

Jason looked around the room and saw a stainless steel stool. He stepped around to the other side of the emergency table and sat down on it while he waited for Kandace to gather her thoughts.

He could not help but notice that in spite of the fresh dressing on the side of her head just back of her eye and over her temple, the woman was very beautiful. Her long auburn hair appeared to be soft and silky, so much so that he had an urge to reach out and touch it. Her complexion was smooth with a few tiny freckles lightly dotting her cheeks and the bridge of her nose. Yet, it was the deep green of her eyes that seemed to capture his attention, eyes that he could see, but could not see him.

"There were two men," she said which quickly drew Jason's attention back to his job. "One of them was fairly short, probably five foot six inches tall, or so. He was not very well educated by the sound of his speech. Oh, he also sounded like he had been drinking, hard liquor from the smell of him."

"Excuse me, but how do you know he was short?"

She smiled. "When you live in a world of darkness where there is just a hint of light, you learn to listen and hear where the sounds are coming from. It often helps you to avoid walking into something, or someone."

"I see," he said immediately wishing that he had just shut up and listened.

"I will never forget their voices. I would know them anywhere."

Jason thought he heard a slight quiver in her voice. He wondered if it was fear of the two men, or anger toward them for what they had done to her and her dog.

"Are you sure that you could identify the two men just by hearing their voices again?"

"Oh yes," she replied without a second of hesitation.

Just then, the door to the room came open. It was Diana pushing a wheelchair. She had come to take Kandace to another room.

"I'm sorry, Lieutenant, but we have to take Miss Clarke to her room now. The doctor would like her to get some rest and it is getting rather late. I'm afraid that visiting hours are over."

"Certainly," he replied as he stood up.

"Lieutenant, ah, Jason?"

"Yes?"

"You will be sure to let me know about Chester as soon as you hear something, won't you?"

"Of course. You get some rest like the doctor ordered. I'll be by in the morning. We can visit some more then."

"Thank you for all you've done," she said as she held out her hand.

Jason looked at her hand for a moment before he reached out and took hold of it. Her hand was small and delicate, yet it had a definite strength to it.

"You're welcome," Jason replied as he stood up.

Jason held her hand longer then what would have been considered to be normal. He let go of her hand and left the emergency room without saying anything more.

Kandace could hear the sound of his footsteps as he walked down the hall toward the exit. Her thoughts quickly turned to thoughts of Lieutenant Barrett, Jason Barrett. The sound of his fading footsteps gave her the impression that he was tall and walked with the confidence of a man who was very sure of himself.

Kandace smiled to herself as she reflected on the sound of his voice. Although his voice was that of a caring man, gentle and reassuring, she was sure that he could be a harsh man if the need should arise.

"What's he like?" Kandace asked as Diana reached out and took hold of her arm.

"I've seen him around here before, but I don't really know the Lieutenant very well. I wouldn't mind getting to know him."

"Is he a handsome man?"

"Yes, very handsome," Diana replied with a smile in her voice.

"Tell me what he looks like."

"Well, he's tall, probably about six two or six three. He has dark brown hair that is slightly wavy with just a hint of gray on the sides. He is well built. You know, broad shoulders, narrow waist."

"What's his face like?"

"Well, he's sort of --."

"No, don't tell me," she interrupted.

Diana did not say any more, she simply smiled as she helped Kandace from the treatment table to the wheelchair. As soon as Kandace was seated, Diana wheeled her out into the hall to the elevator. Diana took her up to the second floor to a private room just a couple of doors from the nurse's station. Once Kandace had gotten into a hospital gown and was settled into the bed, Diana told her goodnight, shut off the light and left her alone.

Kandace lay in the bed with her eyes closed, but she could not fall asleep. Her mind was cluttered with thoughts of Chester and how she was going to get along without him until he recovered. She also thought about a certain Lieutenant.

When she began to think of Lieutenant Barrett, she continued to wonder just what he was really like. She had wanted Diana to tell her what he looked like, but when she asked about what his face was like she suddenly didn't want Diana to tell her. Was it because she was afraid that he would not be as handsome as he sounded to her? Maybe it was because she did not want a picture in her mind of someone she would never hear from again, once the case was solved. Maybe, it was because she hoped that he would let her get close enough to him to allow her to touch his face and see for herself what he looked like.

Time passed slowly for her. She was looking forward to having Lieutenant Barrett visit her again. Gradually, she grew tired as the excitement of the evening wore off and the discomfort of her wounds decreased. Her last thoughts before she slipped into a quiet restful sleep were of Jason and the anticipation of his next visit. Somehow, knowing that he was looking after Chester made it easier for her to relax and get the rest she needed.

* * * *

As Jason drove away from the hospital, his thoughts were of Miss Clarke. He was pleased to find out that she was single. It made it easier for him to admit to himself that he was attracted to her. After all, she was a beautiful woman and he was a normal man who appreciated seeing a beautiful woman. She had a lot of the qualities that he liked in women. She was strong, self reliant, determined, pleasant and very nice looking.

He had started toward home for the night, but suddenly found himself turning onto the street that would take him back to where Kandace had been attacked, and to where he had first met her. As he turned his car into the alley where the men had laid in wait, he stopped. The bright headlights of his car lit up the alley making it easy to see for several hundred feet. He just sat there looking out through the windshield, examining every detail of the alley.

Sitting quietly, he mentally reviewed everything that Kandace had been able to remember. It seemed logical that the two men would have used the alley for their escape route. After all, it provided a quick route to a number of other streets. Jason was convinced that they would have gone down the alley, dumping her briefcase and purse as soon as they had taken anything of value. They would have had to take the time to stop some place nearby to search Kandace's purse and briefcase, which would mean that they probably knew the area well. It would not have been very wise for them to run around carrying a purse and briefcase.

Jason took his foot off the brake and let the car slowly creep down the alley. Using the spotlight on his unmarked police car, he checked out every doorway, every window, and every pile of trash he came across in the alley. When he would come to a Dumpster, he would stop, get out, and shine his flashlight into the Dumpster. He would find almost all of them to be empty. It seemed strange that the Dumpsters were empty, yet there were piles of trash lying around on the ground. He surmised that the trash trucks must have emptied them that day and that they only picked up what was in the

Dumpsters. It seemed that no one ever cleaned up the areas around the Dumpsters. He would push some of the trash around the empty Dumpster with his foot looking for evidence before moving on to the next.

By the time he reached the end of the block, he had found nothing. Before crossing the street, he stopped and looked both ways. He wondered which way the thieves might have gone.

Letting out a sigh of frustration, he looked straight ahead, on down the alley. In the distance, he thought he saw something move. The headlights of his car reflected off something bright, like chrome or metal. When it moved, he realized that he was seeing a shopping cart and someone was pushing it.

He drove across the street and on down the alley. As he got closer, he saw an old lady bending down and going through the trash. Just as he pulled up to a stop, the old lady turned and looked at him. As she stood up, he noticed that she was holding what appeared to be a rather nice looking briefcase.

"You there, hold on," he said as he got out of the car.

"Get away from me," she retorted as she backed away from Jason and quickly moved toward her shopping cart. "I'll call the cops."

"I am the cops, lady" Jason replied as he pulled his badge and ID card out of his inside jacket pocket.

"I didn't steal nothin'," the old lady said sharply.

"I didn't say you did. I want to know where you got that briefcase?"

"I found it," she replied as she wrapped her arms around it and held it close to her chest. "It's mine."

"Where did you find it?"

"I found it over there," she said as she pointed toward some old boxes piled near a Dumpster.

"I'd like to see it."

"You can't have it, it's mine," she said as she held the briefcase behind her as if hiding it would make him not want it any more.

"We can do this the easy way, or we can do this the hard way. Show me the briefcase now, or I'll take it away from you and throw you in jail for hiding evidence."

"You wouldn't?"

"Oh, yes I would. And I'll leave your cart right here where it can be easily found."

"You wouldn't do that to an old lady, would you?"

"Yes, I would. And you know that if you go to jail, someone will come along and take your shopping cart and everything in it."

She looked at Jason and then at her shopping cart. Jason knew that everything the old lady had to her name was in that shopping cart and she was not likely to give it up easily.

Looking back at Jason, she reluctantly held the briefcase out to him. Jason took the briefcase from the woman and looked at it. On the front, were the initials K.R.C., Kandace R. Clarke. He did not know what the 'R' stood for, but he was sure that it was Kandace's briefcase.

"Have you opened it?" he asked.

"No. It's locked, but there's somethin' in it."

"Show me where you found it."

"I told you, right over there," she said again pointing to the pile of boxes. "You going to keep it?"

"Yes."

"Is there a reward for finding it?"

"No. Did you find anything else, like a purse, maybe?"

"No. I didn't find nothin' else, honest."

Jason felt sorry for the old woman. Her clothes were dirty and worn, and there was a spot of dirt under her left eye. She probably hadn't had a decent meal or a bath for some time. He wasn't sure if she was telling him the truth, but he had no reason not to believe her.

"Just one more thing, did you see who dropped the briefcase there?"

"Nope."

Jason just stood there for a couple of seconds looking at the woman, wondering if the woman might be lying to him. It had taken a little convincing, but she had cooperated with him, even if he did have to threaten her. He reached in his wallet, took out a ten-dollar bill and handed it to the woman.

"This is for your trouble. If you happen to remember who dropped the briefcase, or hear anything about two men who robbed a blind woman, give me a call," he said as she reached out and grabbed the bill from him. "I'll even pay for the call, and for any information you can provide."

She looked at the bill, then at Jason. Carefully, she stuffed the bill down the front of the ragged dress, closing her old heavy coat tightly around herself. She turned and began pushing her shopping cart down the alley. She had only gone a few feet when she stopped and turned back toward Jason.

"Will yah pay for the purse?"

"Yes, if it's the right purse. Do you know where it is?"

"No, but I'll be lookin' for it."

Jason could not help but smile as he watched the old woman turn and push her cart on down the alley. He wondered if she knew more than she was telling him, or if she was just trying to figure out how to get more money from him.

As soon as the old woman was out of sight, Jason put the briefcase in his car, grabbed a flashlight and began searching the area around the boxes. After searching through the alley for over an hour, he found nothing. His feet were beginning to feel the cold and he decided to call it a night. He could pick up where he left off in the morning.

There was nothing more Jason could do tonight, so he got back in his car and started for home. As his mind went over all that had happened, he remembered that he had not checked to see how Chester was doing.

As soon as he arrived at his apartment, he called the animal shelter to find out where Chester had been taken. He found out that he had been taken to a local animal hospital for treatment of his injuries, but no one at the animal shelter could tell Jason anything about Chester's condition. He tried to call the animal hospital, but all he got was an answering service that suggested he call in the morning.

Realizing that he would not be able to get any information tonight, he got ready for bed. After climbing into bed, he laid on his back, his hands behind his head. His thoughts once again turned to Kandace. He had no idea why she continued to be on his mind so much, but she did. Maybe, it was because he had held her for so long while he waited for the ambulance. He could still remember the fresh soft scent of her hair as he held her. It was late before he finally drifted off to sleep.

CHAPTER THREE

Jason woke to the very irritating sound of his alarm clock. He felt as if the darn thing went off just minutes after he had finally fallen asleep. He reached over to the bedside table and shut off the alarm with a firm slap of his hand. Rolling onto his back, he tried to rub the sleep from his eyes. He stretched in an effort to wake himself up and prepare himself for the day ahead.

It was not customary for him to set his alarm clock on days when he did not have to report to work. In fact, he usually made it a point to sleep in. However, that morning was different. He had things to do.

As the sleep induced fog cleared from his brain, he remembered that he needed to check on Chester's condition as soon as the animal hospital's office opened. He rolled over and sat up on the side of the bed for a moment before heading for the bathroom. After a warm shower and shave, he dressed in a pair of jeans and a bulky sweatshirt that was casual enough to be comfortable, yet nice enough to look good for a casual visit to the hospital.

He went into the kitchen and put a cup of coffee in the microwave, a piece of bread in the toaster and poured himself a glass of orange juice. Sitting down at the table, he picked up the phone and dialed the number of the animal hospital.

"Dr. Thompson's office, may I help you?" the young female voice on the other end answered.

"This is Lieutenant Barrett of the Fort Collins Police Department. A large German Shepherd was brought into your clinic yesterday evening for treatment of injuries it received during an attack on its owner. The dog's name is Chester and he is a Seeing Eye dog. Can you tell me what the dog's condition is?"

"Yes, Lieutenant. The dog is doing rather well, much better than we had expected. He suffered some pretty severe injuries, but he is expected to be all right; although, it will take awhile for him to completely recover."

"Can you give me some idea as to how long it will be before the dog will be able to be returned to his owner?"

"No, I'm afraid I can't. We will have to wait and see how he responds to treatment. That might take a couple of days. If all goes well, I would think it would be at least a week, possibly longer. Like I said, the dog had some pretty severe injuries."

"Thank you. I'll be in touch with the doctor later," Jason said, then hung up the phone.

A week would be a long time for Kandace to be without her Seeing Eye dog, Jason thought as he spread some peanut butter on his toast. After retrieving his coffee from the microwave, he returned to the table and took a bite of toast as he stared across the room.

He began to wonder how Kandace would get around without her dog. It occurred to him that he had no idea what it must be like for her, not being able to see. He wondered if she had always been blind, or if she had been able to see at one time.

As Jason looked around the room, he decided to try a little experiment. He went to his dresser and got out a handkerchief. He wrapped it around his head, covering his eyes. After making sure that he could not see anything, he stood in the middle of his bedroom and tried to envision where everything was in the room. Carefully, he stumbled his way back to the kitchen and to the table where he sat down. Moving his hands very slowly and carefully, he tried to find the toast and the glass of juice that were on the table.

Jason quickly discovered that his experiment proved to be a little messy when he bumped the glass and spilled some of the juice. He also stuck his fingers in the peanut butter. He even went so far as to attempt to clean up the spilled juice without removing the blindfold from his eyes. Without being able to see, he was not sure if he had gotten it all cleaned up or not.

Just as he was about to give up and remove the blindfold, the doorbell rang. He started toward the door before removing the blindfold completely and ran directly into the corner of the coffee table. He let out a cry of pain as he cracked his shin against the edge of the table, which tripped him and caused him to fall.

"Just a minute," he called out as he sat up and briefly rubbed his shin to help relieve the pain.

Jason's shin still hurt as he picked himself up off the floor and limped to the door. He hesitated for just a second before opening the door in order to regain his composure.

"Oh, hi, Mrs. Hamilton."

"I'm sorry to disturb you, Mr. Barrett, but this letter was left for you. I thought it might be important and that you might need it right away."

Jason stood holding the door to prevent it from opening all the way. He noticed that Mrs. Hamilton was trying very hard to look around him in order to see into the apartment. She had probably heard him stumble over the coffee table and wondered what was going on.

"Thank you, Mrs. Hamilton," he replied as he reached out for the letter.

"You know, you really should find a nice girl," she said as she put the letter in his hand. "You shouldn't live alone, it's not healthy, you know."

"Well, I'm sure you will be happy to know that I'm working on that very problem," he replied with a smile.

A surprised look came over Mrs. Hamilton's face as Jason quickly thanked her again for the letter and closed the door before she had a chance to respond. He smiled to himself because he was sure that his last comment would keep her busy for the rest of the day wondering what he was doing. He glanced at the letter and saw that it was nothing important. Whatever was in the letter could wait. He threw it down on the coffee table on his way back to the kitchen. Right now, he had other things on his mind, for one, Kandace Clarke.

He glanced up at the clock above the kitchen sink and discovered that it was still too early to go to the hospital to see how Kandace was doing. His thoughts turned back to his experiment and how much of a problem it had been for him to get along without sight, even for just a few minutes. He was sure that Kandace would not have as much of a problem as he had. After all, she had been blind for some time and would have adapted to the situation, at least to some degree.

Jason was sure that Kandace would be able to get around her apartment fairly easily without the aid of Chester, but getting to and from work would probably be her biggest problem. He spent a few minutes thinking about it before he decided that

Kandace would certainly have a number of friends who would help her get to and from work.

Jason grew more and more angry as he thought about what those two men had done to her. They didn't just steal her purse and briefcase; they took away her freedom to get around, her independence, and her security. The more he thought about it, the more determined he became to catch them. He decided that he would go back to the alley and continue his search for clues before going to the hospital.

* * * *

Kandace lay motionless on the hospital bed with her eyes closed, but she was not asleep. She had been awake for a while. Her mind was filled with thoughts of Chester and an occasional thought of Lieutenant Barrett.

In her heart, she knew that even if Chester survived his injuries, it would be a long time before he could guide her around again. Even if he did regain his health, would he still be the confident, loving dog she had known for these past years? The big question that remained to be answered was would he ever be able to meet the rigid discipline requirement of a Seeing Eye dog? Kandace had her doubts, and that saddened her.

Tears came to her eyes as she thought about the pain her Chester had suffered at the hands of those two men. Her tears were also for herself and how lonely she would be without him to keep her company, and how quiet it would be in her apartment without him there to talk to.

Kandace had moved to Fort Collins only two years ago and had not made any real close friends that she could count on to help her while Chester was laid up. Her closest friend was Marsha, a fellow employee who was out of town for the weekend.

Kandace had chosen to keep to herself and try to make it on her own. Her family lived several hundred miles away and had tried to discourage her from taking the position she currently held because it required her to move to Fort Collins. She was beginning to wonder if her show of independence had been such a good idea after all that had happened. Kandace wanted to call her parents and tell them about Chester, but she knew that she would get nothing but a big "I told you so" from them. Then they would insist that she move back to Omaha where they could take care of her. To return to Omaha would be to admit that they were right, that she needed someone to "take care of her". It would also take away her independence, something that was very important to her self-esteem.

Her thoughts were suddenly interrupted by the sound of the door to her room opening. Kandace quickly wiped the tears from her eyes. She then heard the sound of the drapes being drawn open and she could see a little light so she knew that the sun was probably shining.

"Good morning," a rather pleasant female voice said. "How are we feeling this morning?"

"I'm fine," she replied with a slight quiver in her voice.

"The doctor should be by to see you in a little while."

"Do you think he will let me go home?"

"Well, your vital signs have been good and your color is good. They do want to run a couple of tests on you this morning; but if everything is all right, I would think that you should be able to go home by this afternoon. Do you have someone who can come and take you home?"

Tears began to come to her eyes again. She had no one who would be able to help her. She suddenly felt very much alone. It would be difficult for her to take the bus, as she was not familiar with the bus routes from the hospital to her apartment house. If she had to change buses and there was no one to help her choose the right bus, she could get lost. The only other option would be for her to call for a cab to take her home. She still had difficulty depending on others to see for her. Chester had been her only trusted friend since she moved there.

"No. I will have to get a cab, I guess."

"Oh."

The sound of the nurse's voice left Kandace wondering if they might keep her longer if she was unable to get a ride home. It even passed through her mind to call Lieutenant Barrett and ask him to take her home, but that thought quickly slipped away. He had been helpful and sounded like a kind man, but he was just doing his duty and probably felt sorry for her. She'd had enough of people feeling sorry for her and didn't need any more of it.

Thinking of Lieutenant Barrett reminded her that he was going to call her and let her know how Chester was getting along. She realized that she had not heard from him and wondered if he had already forgotten about her and her dog.

"Have there been any calls for me?"

"No, I don't believe so. Are you expecting someone to call?"

"I was hoping that Lieutenant Barrett might call and let me know how my dog is doing."

"Your dog?"

"Yes, my Seeing Eye dog. He was hurt yesterday during the attack on me."

"Oh. I didn't know about that. No, he hasn't called yet, but I'm sure he will. It's still early. I will let you know when he calls."

Disappointment filled her senses and she turned her face away from the nurse. Her mind filled with thoughts of Chester again. The first was that

Chester had died, or worse, they had to put him to sleep so that he would not suffer any more pain rather than try to save him. No, it would be worse for her if he lived and could no longer be a friend and companion to her, she thought.

She buried her face in her pillow when she heard the nurse leave her room. Tears flowed from her eyes in almost a steady stream. She could not remember a time when she felt so lonely and so alone, and so in need of a friend. Not since the accident that left her blind had she felt so depressed and saddened by a loss in her life.

After a few minutes, she rolled over and reached out to the bedside table for a tissue. Slowly, she lightly touched everything on the table so as not to knock over anything that might be on the table. Finding the tissues, she took one from the box and wiped her eyes.

Gradually, she began to take control of her emotions. She had had her cry, now it was time to pull herself together and take charge of her life again, she thought. There was no doubt in her mind that it would be difficult to get along without Chester's help, but she could do it. She had to do it because the alternative was not an option to her way of thinking. To return to Omaha meant failing to be able to be on her own. She could not allow herself to fail. She could not give up, no matter what.

She heard the door to her room open again and she looked toward the door. The footsteps where those of a man in hard street shoes.

"Well, Miss Clarke, how are we doing this morning?"

"Fine." she replied with a hint of a question in her voice.

"I'm sorry. I'm Doctor Petersen."

"Will I be able to leave soon?"

"Let's see," he replied as he reached out and took her by the wrist. "Does your head still hurt?"

"Just a little. Mostly where the stitches are."

"Do you have a headache?"

"No. Just a little discomfort."

"Well, Miss Clarke, I want to run a couple of tests."

"What kind of tests?"

"I want to take a couple of x-rays and generally check you over before I release you. If everything goes as I expect it will, you should be able to leave this afternoon. The nurse tells me that you will have to take a taxi to get home, is that right?"

"Yes," she replied feeling a little anxiety that he might be reluctant to let her go.

"I have been getting around quite well without anyone's help for some time. I'm sure that I can get home by myself," she said with a little more of a defensive tone in her voice than she had intended.

"Oh, I'm sure you can. I was just hoping that there might be someone who could look in on you from time to time over the weekend. After that, I don't see any reason why you couldn't carry on your daily activities as usual."

"I'm sure that my landlady would be happy to look in on me."

"Great. I don't see any reason for you to stay any longer than necessary. I will sign a release for you and you can leave as soon as I have completed the tests and have the results."

"Thank you."

"I do want you to stop in the emergency room in a week to get the stitches taken out and to give us a chance to see how you are doing."

"All right," she replied.

"I'll send the nurse in as soon as we're ready to do the tests."

"Thank you."

Kandace could hear the sound of the doctor's shoes on the hard floor as he left the room. She was a little concerned about the test. It had been a long time since she had been in a hospital. The last time was after the accident that had left her blind.

It wasn't long before the nurse came in to take her for the tests. As she stood up, she felt a little dizzy and was glad that there was a wheelchair to sit in. The nurse wheeled her to x-ray department where several x-rays including a skull series were taken. They also took a blood test that they said was routine before she was returned to her room.

"You can relax for now. It will take a little while for the results of the tests to come back," the nurse said as she helped Kandace back onto the bed.

Kandace did not feel comfortable in the hospital gown and wanted to get into her own clothes. She was not familiar with the hospital room and was not sure where they had put her clothes. She sat up on the side of the bed. With what little light she could make out from the windows, she had a pretty good idea where the closet might be.

She slid off the bed and stood up. As soon as she stood, the side of her head began to throb a little and she felt a little unsteady. She leaned against the bed for a moment until the light-headedness seemed to go away. Just as she was about to feel her way across the room, the door opened.

"Miss Clarke, where are you going?" the nurse said.

"The doctor said that I could go home. I was just trying to find my clothes."

"Let me help you."

"If you would just lay them out on the foot of the bed, I can manage."

"You sure you don't need any help?"

"No. I can manage," Kandace repeated firmly.

"By the way, there's a gentleman out in the hall waiting to see you. I told him that you were getting back from x-ray, and that it would be a minute or two before you would be ready to have company."

"Who is it?"

"He said his name is Jason Barrett."

Kandace suddenly felt a rush of happiness flow through her. It was difficult for her to understand the feelings that she was experiencing just from the sound of his name. She could not have described her feelings, but they filled her with pleasure and a kind of whimsical feeling along with a feeling of relief. He had come to see her again, just as he had promised.

Suddenly, she realized that he might have come to tell her that she would never feel the confident tug of Chester on his lead as he took her from one place to another. She would never feel Chester's smooth, soft fur as she ran her hand over him. Leaning against the bed, she let out a long slow sigh in an effort to prepare herself for the worst.

"Are you all right?" the nurse asked.

"Yes. Would you mind telling Mr. Barrett that I will be out in a minute, please?"

"Sure. Your clothes are on the end of the bed."

Kandace waited until she heard the door close before she took off the hospital gown and she started to get dressed in her own clothes. She didn't have any lipstick; however, the hospital had provided her with a comb. At least she could comb out some of the snarls.

As she dressed and combed her hair, her mind filled with thoughts of Chester again, and what her life would be like without him. She was convinced that Jason had come to tell her that Chester was dead. Tears once again filled her eyes, but she could not help it. Her life without Chester would never be the same.

As soon as she felt she could face Jason and the news that he was surely bringing, she wiped the tears from her face and straightened her shoulders. Making a firm resolution not to cry in front of anyone, she felt around on the bed for the button to summon help. Finding the button, she pushed it, then sat down on the edge of the bed and waited.

CHAPTER FOUR

After going back over the area where Miss Clarke had been attacked, Jason once again drove through the alley. He didn't know what he expected to find. Maybe he didn't expect to find anything, but he still had the feeling that he might have overlooked something. He had to look again, just in case.

He was in the second block when he saw the old bag lady that he had talked to last night. She was waving her arms around as if she wanted him to stop. Jason pulled up beside the lady's shopping cart and rolled down the window.

"Good morning," Jason said with a smile.

"Same to yah. Did you say you was lookin' for a purse last night?"

"Yes. Did you find it?"

"No, not yet, but I will. How much is it worth to yah?"

"Well, let me put it this way. It could be worth as much as twenty dollars if you find it and give it to me right away. But, if you have it and keep it from me, it could be worth a few days in jail. Now, we wouldn't want that, would we?"

"No, sir. I'll keep lookin'."

"You do that. I'll be in touch," Jason assured her as he rolled up the window and drove on down the alley.

He glanced in his rear view mirror and saw the old lady watching him as he drove away. Just from the way she acted, Jason wondered if the old woman had any idea who it was that attacked Miss Clarke and her dog. It was hard to tell what some of these old street people really knew. In their own area, they often knew more about what was going on than some of the people that owned houses there. He decided that he would have to have another talk with her later.

Jason glanced at his watch and decided that it was late enough that he could go to the hospital to see Miss Clarke. He pulled out of the alley and turned down the street. He was not very far from the hospital and arrived just a little after ten. He parked in the reserved parking space for official vehicles and went inside to inquire about Miss Clarke.

After talking to the duty nurse, Jason stood at the nurse's station leaning against the counter. He looked down the hall toward Kandace's room while he waited for the nurse to tell her that he was there.

"Excuse me, but I understand you are waiting for Miss Clarke?"

Jason turned to see a rather pleasant looking older gentleman in a white smock standing next to him. He had been so preoccupied with his thoughts that he had not seen him approach the nurse's station. The man had a patient's chart in his hand and the nametag on his smock indicated that he was a doctor.

"Yes, yes I am. Is there a problem?"

"No, not at all. I'm Doctor Petersen. I overheard you ask about Miss Clarke. Miss Clarke seems to be doing quite well. If the tests that we ran this morning are negative, she should be able to go home."

"I'm glad to hear that."

"However, I am a little concerned about her," Doctor Petersen continued. "The nurse tells me that Miss Clarke lives alone, and that her Seeing Eye dog was injured in the attack on her last night."

"That's correct. The dog will recover, but it will take some time."

I see," the doctor replied. "I would feel much better about releasing her if I knew for sure that there was someone who could look in on her from time to time over the weekend. Just as a precaution, you understand. She said that her landlady would look in on her, but I feel a little uncomfortable with that arrangement. If I was sure that her landlady would indeed look in on her several times a day, I would feel much better about releasing her."

"If it will make you feel better, doctor, I'll look in on her over the weekend to make sure that she's fine."

"That does make me feel better. She should be able to return to work on Monday, but I suppose without her dog it will be difficult for her to get around."

"I would think so."

As Jason watched the doctor sign the release order in Kandace's chart, he wondered what it was that had made him volunteer so quickly to look after Miss Clarke. Up until now, he had always made it a point not to get involved with other people's personal problems, especially those he was involved with on a professional basis.

It quickly passed through his mind that he might care about the woman, but he quickly pushed that thought from his mind. He justified his decision to look out for her as no big deal. After all he did have the weekend off, and his only plans were to watch a couple of football games anyway. It would give him something else to do, otherwise he would end up spending the whole weekend in front of the television. It suddenly occurred to him that Miss Clarke might not like the idea of him barging into her life without asking first.

Just then, the door to Kandace's room opened and the nurse came out. She smiled as she approached him at the nurse's station. "She is ready to see you, Lieutenant."

"Thank you," Jason replied as he started down the hall.

When he arrived at her door, he knocked lightly before stepping into the room.

"Come in," Kandace said as she turned toward the door.

"Good morning. How are you doing?"

"I'm doing fine. As soon as I get the results of some tests they did this morning, I can go home."

Jason looked at her as she sat on the edge of the bed. She looked as if she was ready to leave the hospital now. She must have the same confidence in what the tests would show as the doctor, he thought.

"Well, I have some news for you about your dog."

"Is it good news, I hope?"

"Well, yes. I think you will like what you hear considering how badly Chester was hurt. The veterinarian tells me that Chester is going to be fine. He was hurt pretty badly, but he will be able to be home in about a week, or so. I guess the bad news is that he will not be able to help you get around for at least the better part of a month."

"Thank you. I'll never be able to repay you for your kindness," she said as she reached out a hand to Jason.

Jason stepped up next to the bed and took hold of her hand. Her hand felt soft and warm as he gently squeezed it. She looked up at him and he thought that he could see tears in her eyes. He held her hand longer than would have been considered necessary, but he didn't want to let go of her.

"Ah, well, ah," Jason stumbled for something to say as he finally let go of her hand. "Oh, do you have someone coming to take you home?"

"No. I - I was going to call a cab."

She smiled as if she could see him standing in front of her.

"Well, if you don't mind, I would be glad to see you home."

"Oh, that won't be necessary. I don't want to impose. You've done so much already."

"It's really no trouble, besides I still have a few things that I would like to talk to you about."

"Oh. In that case, very well. I still have to wait for the results of the tests."

"Okay. How about we go down to the cafeteria for a bite to eat while we wait?"

"Sure, but I don't have any money. My purse was stolen, remember?"

"I do remember. This will be on me."

"I think we should tell the nurse where we are going, don't you?"

"I'll take care of that. Be right back."

Jason left the room to tell the nurse where they were going. The nurse just smiled and told Jason to have her back in about an hour. He agreed and went back to Kandace's room.

Jason took hold of her hand and wrapped it around his arm. She held his arm as he walked her to the elevator. They didn't say anything as they rode down to the floor where the cafeteria was located, they were both deep in their own thoughts. Jason guided her off the elevator to a table in the cafeteria where they sat down.

"What would you like?" Jason asked.

"Just a sandwich, ham and cheese if they have it, and a cup of coffee."

"Okay, one ham and cheese with coffee, coming up. Oh, how do you like your coffee?"

"Black, please."

"Black it is."

Jason got up and went through the line to get them both a sandwich. Kandace sat waiting at the table. It was difficult for her to believe that she could be enjoying the stranger's company after what had happened last night. Although she enjoyed being with him, she knew that he would have to return to business. After all, he was a policeman, and he did have his work to do.

"There you are, one ham and cheese sandwich dead ahead, and a cup of hot black coffee at two o'clock," Jason said as he set the plate and cup on the table.

"You must have helped blind people before."

"No, not really. I've just seen other people help them."

Jason sat down across from her and watched her as she found the food right where he said it would be. He knew that he would have to question her about last night, but he hesitated to begin.

"I'm sure you have a lot of questions to ask me."

"Ah, yes I do," he stumbled looking for the right thing to say.

"Well?"

"I was wondering if you would mind if I look in on you over the weekend?"

"What?" she asked with surprise.

"Well, the doctor is concerned about you being alone, and he wanted someone to look in on you."

"I told him that my landlady would look in on me," she stated angrily.

"I'm sorry. I didn't mean to butt in."

"Do you think I'm helpless, Lieutenant?"

"No, of course not," he retaliated angrily. "I think that I would like to see you, but if that's too much for you to handle, I'll just see you home as I promised."

Kandace suddenly realized that she was taking out her frustration with all those who seemed to think that she was helpless on Jason. Her anger toward him was uncalled for and certainly unjustified. After all he had done nothing but try to be helpful.

"I'm sorry, Lieutenant."

"So am I."

"I mean it. It's just that everyone thinks that I need to be taken care of because I am blind."

"Listen. You are quite capable of taking care of yourself. I know that and you know that. What happened to you last night could have happened just as easily to a sighted person with the same results."

"Thank you," she said with an apologetic tone in her voice.

"Finish up. I promised to have you back in an hour."

After they finished their meal, Jason guided her back to her room where they waited for the doctor. The doctor told her that all of the tests were negative and that she could go home as soon as she signed out.

Within a few minutes the nurse came into Kandace's room with a wheelchair. Knowing that it was the rules, Kandace sat down in the chair and the nurse wheeled her to the elevator. Jason stood next to her as they all waited for the elevator doors to open. He glanced down and noticed that she was facing straight ahead as if looking right at the elevator door.

Just then the elevator door opened and the nurse pushed Kandace into the elevator. Jason followed along behind. When the elevator stopped, Kandace was pushed over to a window that had a sign above it that read, "Check out". With Jason's help to read the forms and explain what they were for, Kandace signed her insurance forms and was released from the hospital.

Kandace was then wheeled through the doors. After being helped out of the wheelchair by the nurse, Jason took her by the hand and slipped it around his arm. He began walking across the parking lot to his car with Kandace hanging onto his arm. He was feeling a little uncomfortable, as he had never led a blind person around before that day. He was not sure how fast to walk, or how much help he should try to be. It was different inside the building, the floors were flat with no steps or curbs to step over.

Once they got to the car, he opened the door and helped her in. Closing the door, he went around to the other side. He got in and started the car. Leaving the parking lot, he drove down the street toward the section of town where Kandace lived.

"I would like to thank you for taking me home. I didn't like the idea of riding in a cab."

"That's quite all right."

"You said you wanted to talk to me, Lieutenant. This would be as good a time as any."

"Yes. First of all, I would like you to feel free to call me, Jason."

A soft smile came over her face as she appeared to be staring out the windshield of the car. "All right, Jason. And secondly?"

"I was able to find your briefcase last night."

"Oh. Where did you find it?"

"An old bag lady had it. She said she found it in a Dumpster about two blocks from where you were attacked. Was there anything of value in it?"

"I take it that you found it empty."

"No, as a matter of fact I bought it from the bag lady who found it. It was still locked. It didn't appear to have been opened. I have it in the back seat."

"You bought it from her?" she said with surprise.

"It was really a donation so she could get a good meal. I didn't really have to pay for it."

"That was nice of you."

"She'll probably buy a bottle of cheap wine with the money."

"Probably. All that is in my briefcase are some papers from work. Nothing of any value to anyone except me. It would take a lot of work to replace them, but it would not be impossible," she explained. "Besides, not many people would be able to read most of them anyway, they are written in Braille."

"I'll bet they would have been disappointed if they had opened your briefcase. I haven't found your purse, yet. Did you have anything of value in it?"

"Nothing that can't be replaced. I will have to call my credit card companies to have my cards canceled and replaced. I'll have to get a new ID card. Oh, there was some money in it, maybe seventy-five dollars and my keys."

Jason glanced over toward her as she continued to mentally review all the items that had been in her purse. She did not seem to be too upset by the missing valuables, but Jason made a mental note of the things she said she was missing. The one item that concerned him the most was the fact that the thieves had her keys, keys to her apartment and the address of her apartment.

Jason pulled his car up in front of Kandace's apartment building and stopped. He helped her from the car and up the steps to the front door. As they entered the building, Jason noticed that there was not a security door at the entrance to the building.

"I can find my way from here," Kandace said as she reached out and touched the wall. She didn't want him to go, but she had taken a great deal of his time already.

"That's all right, I'll walk you to your apartment if you don't mind."

Mind? She didn't mind at all. She liked the sound of his voice and the concern he showed her. It would be nice to have someone to talk to, especially Jason. She had found herself thinking about him a lot since last night.

"I'll have to stop at the manager's apartment so I can get a new key to my apartment."

She once again took him by the arm and followed him down the hall. When they got to the manager's apartment, he reached out and knocked on the door. It was just a matter of a few seconds before an elderly gentleman opened the door and looked first at Jason and then at Kandace.

"Miss Clarke! What happened to you?"

"I had a little accident," she replied with a note of embarrassment. "This is Lieutenant Barrett with the police department. My purse was taken last night and the keys to my apartment were in my purse. Would you be so kind as to get me another key?"

"Certainly, just one minute."

Kandace smiled up at Jason while they waited for Mr. Stockwell to get a key. She felt secure holding onto his arm. When Mr. Stockwell returned, he again looked at Jason and then handed him the key.

"Thank you," Jason said as he took the key.

"Yes, thank you, Mr. Stockwell," Kandace added.

"Your apartment?"

"It's apartment six on the second floor. We can take the stairs if you like," she said as she hung onto Jason's arm.

Jason led her down the hall to the stairs. He carefully turned the corner, but stopped when he got to the steps.

"First step," he said a little unsure of just how to help her from there.

As she stepped up on the first step, she smiled. "You make a very good Seeing Eye dog."

"I guess that's a pretty good compliment considering I haven't been properly trained for the job."

"Oh, I'm sorry. That must have sounded terrible. I didn't mean it to sound like that," she said as her face began to turn red with embarrassment.

"It's okay," he said with a soft laugh that seemed to ease her embarrassment.

When they reached the top of the stairs, he let Kandace sort of lead him. She seemed to know her way around the apartment building very well, but then why wouldn't she, she lived there.

As they approached the door to apartment six, Jason noticed that the door was slightly ajar. He slowed his pace and Kandace slowed with him. Her grip on his arm tightened slightly as if she knew that there was something wrong, but she remained silent and took her cue from Jason.

"What is it?" she asked in a whisper.

Jason didn't respond to her question right away. Instead he gently, but firmly pushed her behind him and up against the wall.

"Are you in the habit of leaving the door to your apartment open?" he asked softly.

"No, of course not."

"Well, someone did. Wait here. I'm going to make sure that there's no one in there."

Jason released her arm, reached behind his back and pulled his pistol out of his belt. Cautiously, he moved along the wall toward the door. When he was next to the door, he reached out and slowly pushed the door open. Looking into the apartment, he saw that someone had ransacked the place. The cushions from the sofa and chair were out in the middle of the room, drawers had been pulled out of a desk and the contents dumped on the floor and a couple of table lamps were tipped over.

Carefully he stepped into the room. There was no one there. He carefully worked his way through each of the rooms searching the apartment. He went into the kitchen, her bedroom and the extra bedroom. All were in the same condition as the living room, trashed. Whoever had done it was gone, but with what was yet to be determined.

Kandace stood against the wall where Jason had left her, unable to move. She listened carefully for any sound that would give her a clue to what was happening, but she heard nothing. Just minutes before she had been feeling safe and secure, but right now she was afraid and worried for Jason. The fact that he was a policeman did little to help relieve her concerns for his safety.

Jason took one last look around the apartment as he put his pistol back in his belt. He went back out into the hall and found Kandace leaning against the wall with her hands over her mouth. It was clear that she was frightened.

"I'm sorry, but your apartment has been broken into and ransacked. I better call the police," he said as he put his arm around her shoulders.

As she took her hands away from her face and turned in Jason's arms, she buried her face into his shoulder. Tears flowed freely from her eyes as her feelings of fear and panic mixed together to overwhelm her senses. Her private life and the place she lived had been invaded by strangers twice in less than twenty-four hours.

Her body quivered slightly as she thought about what would have happened if she had been able to come home last night, or if she had come home alone earlier today. She might have run right into the thieves again, and that thought frightened her even more.

"Do you have any friends where you can stay for a little while?" he asked as he held her in his arms.

"No," she replied with a sigh. "My best friend is out of town for the weekend."

"Is there any one else you could stay with?"

"No," she replied, her voice showing how frightened she was.

Jason could not help but feel just a little bit sorry for her. First of all, she gets beat up by a couple of thugs who steal her purse, her briefcase and injure her dog, and now trash her apartment. The first thing that came to Jason's mind was it was the same thugs. They had her purse, which would give them her address. They also had her keys that would give them easy access to her apartment.

Jason suddenly realized that he liked holding her. He wasn't sure if it was the fact that she was a beautiful woman who needed his shoulder to lean on, or if it was the fact that it had been a long time since he had held a woman in his arms. Whatever the reason, he liked it.

"Well, you can't stay here."

"But what am I supposed to do?"

The defeat and frustration that she was feeling were clear in the tone of her voice.

With Jason's arms around her, she could feel his strength. That along with the closeness of him gradually evaporated her fears and helped to make her feel sheltered from the outside world once again. A feeling that she had not experienced since she moved from Omaha.

She had been able to get around fairly easily with Chester, but it was the first time that she felt the need to be protected. It was an unfamiliar feeling for her, but considering the frightening things that had happened in the past 24 hours, she supposed that it was quite normal.

Jason gently turned her and wrapped his arm around her shoulders as he led her back to the manager's apartment where he called the police. When the police arrived, Jason left Kandace with the manager while he joined in the search of Kandace's apartment for clues and fingerprints.

Kandace sat quietly in a large overstuffed chair while she waited for Jason to return. She found herself wondering what she would do. There was no way that she could bring herself to go back into her apartment. The thought of being alone in that apartment sent a cold chill down her spine.

Tears came to her eyes as she once again felt the loneliness of having no one to turn to for help. She silently prayed for Jason to return and take her away from there.

CHAPTER FIVE

The loneliness that was slowly consuming Kandace's thoughts was causing her to feel cold and apprehensive. The large overstuffed chair, although very comfortable, did little to help comfort her. Her world had been turned upside down by muggers and it was now filled with strangers. Nothing seemed to be familiar any more, nothing seemed right.

The only thing Kandace knew for sure was that she would not be able to return to her apartment even if the locks on the doors were changed. She would never be able to think of her apartment as the safe haven it had been for her from the day she had moved into it with Chester.

Wrapping her arms around herself in an effort to feel warm and to help herself regain some control of her shattered nerves, she began to question the wisdom of her decision to seek her independence by coming to Fort Collins. All the adjustments that she had to make when she suddenly went from a seeing person to a blind person, and the adjustments she had to make when she came there to make her own way, somehow seemed insignificant now.

"Would you like a cup of coffee, Miss Clarke?"

"What?" Mr. Stockwell's interruption of her thoughts had startled her.

"Would you like some coffee?"

"Yes, thank you."

Mr. Stockwell held out a mug of coffee with one hand and gently guided her hand to the mug with the other. As soon as she touched the warm mug, she wrapped her fingers around it in the hope that it would provide her with some small measure of warmth and comfort from the chilling sensations that she had been experiencing.

As she slowly sipped at the hot liquid, her thoughts returned to Jason. It may have been the warmth of the coffee, or her thoughts of Jason's pleasant voice and caring manner, or the fact that he was a police officer that helped her feel better. Whatever it was, she slowly began to feel less frightened and less chilled by the events of the past day. There was something about Jason that seemed to calm her nerves, although she knew little or nothing about him.

"Miss Clarke?"

"Yes, Mr. Stockwell."

"I will change the lock on your apartment door first thing in the morning."

The soft apologetic tone of Mr. Stockwell's voice did not do a thing to help convince Kandace that changing the lock was going to make her feel more secure in that apartment. She knew he was trying his best, but the thought of returning to her apartment caused her chest to tighten. She put her hand to her chest as a sensation of panic raised within her.

She didn't know how to respond to Stockwell's words. Several thoughts quickly passed through her mind, but none of them seemed to be appropriate when she tried to put them into words. Nothing she could think of could express how she felt right now. Even the thought of telling him that she would have to move seemed unacceptable.

Suddenly, there was a knock on the door that caused Kandace to jump. A small amount of the hot liquid splashed on her hand. She quickly passed the mug to her other hand and wiped the few drops of coffee off her hand onto her slacks, all the while listening to the sounds of Mr. Stockwell's shoes as he walked across the room and opened the door.

"Oh, Lieutenant. Please come in."

"Thank you."

The sound of Jason's voice caused a sudden spark of elation within Kandace. It happened so quickly that she hardly noticed it herself, but it was there. It was difficult for her to describe what she felt when she heard his voice, but it was almost as if his presence was all she needed to dispel her anxieties and to calm her nerves.

"How are you doing?" Jason asked as he walked over to Kandace and stood in front of her.

"Much better now," she replied as she looked up toward him.

"Could you excuse us for a minute, Mr. Stockwell? I need to talk to Miss Clarke, privately."

The fact that he had called her Miss Clarke, and the serious tone of his voice, gave Kandace the distinct feeling that what he had to say was not going to be pleasant.

"Certainly, Lieutenant. I'll be in the kitchen if you need me."

Jason watched Mr. Stockwell as he left the room. As soon as he was gone, Jason turned and looked into the most beautiful pair of emerald green eyes he had ever seen. He hesitated as he looked at her. If only those beautiful eyes could see him, he thought with a pang of regret.

"What is it, Jason?"

Her question brought him quickly back to reality. He wasn't sure how he was going to tell her, but it was necessary.

"Miss Clarke, we believe that the same men that attacked you on the street yesterday, were the same ones that broke into your apartment last night."

The look on Kandace's face suddenly turned pale as if she was going into shock. Somehow she knew that both incidents involved the same men, but hearing it made it more real, more personal, and more frightening.

"Are you all right?" The tone of Jason's voice made it clear that he was concerned about her present state of mind.

"Yes," she replied after a deep breath and a long sigh.

She was confused and wasn't sure what to do, but she had to do something. It took her a minute or two to gather her thoughts and regain her composure.

"What does my apartment look like?" she asked reluctantly.

"I'm sorry, but they made a mess of it."

Slowly, a small tear came to her eye as the events of the past 24 hours began to overwhelm her. It would be an almost impossible task for her to clean it up without some help, but who could she trust enough to help her put it back in order.

"We are done in your apartment. We were able to find a couple of fingerprints, but I don't know how much good they will be. I know this doesn't help much, but if you would like, I can help you clean up your apartment."

The sound of his voice told her that he was sincere in his offer to help, but then he had sounded sincere from the very first time they met on that cold dark street. She wanted to accept his offer, but she just couldn't bring herself to go into that apartment, not yet anyway.

"I - - I can't," she said as she put her hands over her face. "I just can't."

Jason knelt down beside the chair and reached out to her. He put his arms around her shoulders and drew her close to him in an effort to console her.

It was not the first time that Jason had seen the victim of a robbery who was afraid to return to their home or apartment immediately after it had been ransacked. From his experience as a policeman, he had a pretty good idea what she must be going through. He was sure that it must be doubly hard for Kandace because of the added loss of her dog to keep her company.

He had more to tell her, but he felt it could wait until she was better able to handle it. Right now, it would be best to make sure that she was protected, at least until they had a chance to catch her attackers.

"Do you have some place you can go for a little while, some place where you can be with someone, at least until your friend returns?"

She raised her face from his shoulder and looked in his direction. After a big sigh, she wiped the tears from her eyes.

"No. I have nowhere to go."

"Would you like me to stay with you for awhile?"

"I can't ask you to do that, you've done too much already. It's just that I can't deal with this now. I'm just too exhausted to cope with it."

Still touching her arm with his hand, Jason sat back on his heels and looked at her. He knew better than to get personally involved. Even as a rookie policeman, he had been told time and time again not to get personally involved. My God, how many times had he seen the emotional problems that it caused when other officers in his department got personally involved with the victim of a crime? But there was something special about her that compelled him to go against his better judgment.

Sure he was feeling sorry for her, who wouldn't? But it was not because she was blind. She had been through a great deal over the past twenty-four hours and she was holding up better than he had expected, better than a lot of sighted people would.

"Well, ah, listen, ah, you need some place to get some rest and a chance to get away from here for a while. Some place where you can think things out without a lot of pressure. I don't want you to take this the wrong way, but - ah - well. Oh hell, I'll just say it. I don't have any plans for today. If you would like to come over to my apartment for the afternoon, you would certainly be welcome."

"I - - I wouldn't want to put you out on my account."

"You wouldn't be putting me out. Besides, you would be able to get some rest, and it would give you some time to think. What do you say?"

"I don't know."

"Look, I know this is a bit unusual, but I do have a very comfortable sofa. I know. I've spent a few nights on it myself. You're welcome to use it."

A soft smile came over her face as she reached out and found Jason's arm only inches from her hand. She touched his arm lightly and then squeezed it gently. She wanted to accept his offer, but she was hesitant.

Kandace tried to run her options through her head, but quickly discovered that she didn't have very many choices that seemed acceptable. She could stay in her apartment, or she could go to a motel or hotel at least for the night, or she could go with Jason to his apartment. Those were her options as she saw them.

The idea of staying in her apartment was out of the question. Going to a motel and sitting around alone was not much more appealing. Although the motel would be less frightening than staying in her apartment, it would be equally as lonely. At least if she went with Jason, she would have someone to talk to who would at least try to understand what she was going through. Right now, she needed to be with someone, and preferably with someone who would understand. The last thing she wanted was to be alone, and who better to be with than a policeman?

"If you're sure that I won't be a problem for you," she said, still not sure that her decision was the right one.

"No problem at all," he replied with a slight sound of relief. "We can go to your apartment and get whatever you need for the day."

The thought of going back to her apartment for even a short time sent a chill through her. Giving it a second thought, it might not be so bad with Jason there with her.

"What about tonight?" she asked cautiously.

"What about it? You're certainly welcome to stay the night if you want."

"Won't people talk if I stay overnight in your apartment?"

"Oh, I see. I guess you're right. I do have a reputation to maintain, but we'll just have to chance it."

Kandace liked the light airy sound of his voice and the way he made her feel. The soft almost inaudible chuckle that his voice seemed to carry to her ears was reassuring. It was just the thing she needed to hear to pick up her spirits.

"Oh, I just thought of something," Jason said with a hint of devilishness in his voice.

"What's that?"

"Mrs. Hamilton will be ecstatic to learn that I have a woman in my apartment."

"Who is Mrs. Hamilton?"

"She's my landlady. She spends a great deal of time worrying about my love life. In fact, she even brings me my mail from time to time so she can check up on me. I think she does it just to see if I have any women friends staying the night."

"You're kidding?"

"No, I'm not," he said trying to sound very serious. "Why, just this morning she told me that I should find some nice girl, and that I shouldn't live alone. 'It's not healthy', she told me."

"Are you serious?"

"Yes. You will love her. She's really very nice. A bit nosey, but nice.

Taking a more serious tone as he stood up, Jason said, "Let's go up to your apartment and get what you need, then we can go to my place and you can meet Mrs. Hamilton for yourself."

He couldn't miss the sudden change in the expression on her face when he mentioned going back to her apartment. She hesitated, then forced a smile. Going back to her apartment was something that she was going to have to do sooner or later, but she would have preferred later. However, as long as Jason was with her, she was sure that she could manage to return long enough to get the few things that she would need.

Jason took her by the hand and helped her stand. She stood up and allowed him to guide her out of Mr. Stockwell's apartment, down the hall to the stairs and up to her apartment.

With each step closer to the apartment, Kandace grew more anxious. When they arrived at her apartment, Jason unlocked the door and led her inside. As she stepped into the apartment, her breath caught in her throat and she could hardly move.

"The place is kind of a mess," he said as he looked at her and waited for her to try to regain control of herself.

He stood silently holding her hand and squeezing it gently to reassure her that he was with her. Jason could not imagine what it must be like for her. He decided to get the things she would need and get her out of there as soon as possible.

"If you wait right here, I'll gather up what you need, but you are going to have to tell me what you want and help me find it," he said reassuringly.

She hesitated for a moment before saying anything.

"There's a small suitcase in the closet."

Jason found the suitcase, but it was not in the closet. It was lying on the floor of the bedroom with most of the other items that had been in the closet. He picked it up and set it on the bed.

"Okay. Now, all you have to do is tell me what you want and I'll pack it for you. I must warn you that I'm not very good at packing. When I pack, things tend to get wrinkled."

She forced a smile at his effort to make things a little lighter as she tried to think about what she would like packed. For just a second, she thought that maybe it was just as well that she couldn't see the cluttered rooms of her apartment.

She began describing different articles of clothing that she would like and Jason gathered them up. From the choices that she made, it was clear to Jason that she was going for comfort rather than style. She had picked out things like jeans, sweatshirts and comfortable shoes. That suited Jason just fine. He was not planning on anything special for the weekend, anyway. He wanted her to feel comfortable and relaxed while she was in his apartment.

When it came time for Kandace to ask Jason to pack her undergarments, she felt a little embarrassed. She thought about forgetting them, but although she could get along without a bra, she would still need clean panties.

Jason noticed her hesitation. A quick glance at the suitcase made him realize that about all that was left to pack were her so called "unmentionables", and toilet articles. He smiled to himself and decided that there was a good way to relieve her embarrassment.

"Did I tell you that I grew up with three sisters?"

"No," she answered, wondering what he was getting at.

"Well, having grown up with girls around, I think I can figure out pretty much the rest of what you'll need," he said in a casual tone trying very hard to make it sound as if it was no big deal.

She didn't say anything, but the look of relief on her face was enough for Jason. Jason smiled to himself and continued to gather the items that Kandace would need.

Kandace suddenly had an unusual feeling come over her. It had not occurred to her to object to Jason going through her personal belongings even though he was not much more than a stranger to her. Yet, it had upset her a great deal to know that some stranger had been in her apartment. She was sure that the reason for the unusual feeling was the thought that she was going to spend the night at Jason's apartment, an almost total stranger. It also occurred to her that she might be making a mistake by going with him.

Without saying any more, Jason went into the bathroom to finish packing. He added a comb and brush, as well as her toothbrush, cologne and what few other necessary items he felt that she might need or want.

As he returned to the bedroom and zipped up the suitcase, he glanced up at her. There was a strange look on her face, but he couldn't quite figure it out. He wondered if maybe she was having second thoughts.

"Is something wrong?" he asked, his concern for her showing in his voice.

"Ah, well, no, I guess not," she stammered hesitantly.

"I'm sorry. I didn't mean to be so thoughtless. Would you feel more comfortable if I took you to a motel instead of to my place?" he said trying to understand what she must be going through.

"No," she replied softly, but not very convincingly.

"It is difficult for me to understand what you are going through. Things have happened so fast for you. If you would prefer to go some place else for the rest of today and for tonight, I will certainly understand."

"Thank you for at least trying to understand."

"Tell you what. You come over to my place for the afternoon. If by this evening you want to go to a motel or if you would prefer to stay with a policewoman tonight, I will arrange it. Is that fair?"

"Yes," she replied with a smile, somewhat relieved by his offer to provide her with a policewoman.

"Good, then let's go."

Jason picked up the suitcase, then reached out and took her by the hand. With her arm wrapped around his, he led her out of her apartment and down the hall. After a quick stop to remind Mr. Stockwell to be sure to change the lock on the door, he led Kandace out of the building to his car.

CHAPTER SIX

As Jason got into his car and Kandace heard the door shut, she once again wondered if she had made the right decision. It was not like her to go off with a man she knew little or nothing about. The fact that he was a policeman, that he seemed to be very concerned about her and that he had a sense of humor, did not outweigh the fact that she did not really know him.

Although she once again doubted the wisdom of her decision to go with him, she could not ignore the overriding feeling of being safe with him. It was a feeling that she had not felt so strongly with anyone else since before the accident that caused her blindness. Kandace wondered what it could be about him that made her feel so safe. Was the secure feeling due to the fact that she missed Chester, and that she was using Jason as a substitute? Possibly. Was it her renewed suspicion of all strangers and her desire to have someone close by who could protect her? Another possibility. Did she feel guarded, therefore safe, because Jason was a police officer, or was it because he was simply nice to her? Whatever it was that gave her these strange feelings about him, they seemed to help her realize that being with Jason was somehow right for her.

Jason looked over at her and quickly saw the troubled look on her face. She looked worried about something, but he didn't know what it was that troubled her. His first thought was that she had been through so much in such a short time that it would be enough to trouble anyone. For some reason, that did not seem to satisfy Jason's curiosity.

"Is there anything you would like to talk to me about?"

"What?" she replied, her thoughts suddenly disturbed by his question.

"Well, you look a little worried. I thought you might want to talk about it."

"Oh. I was just thinking," she said as she turned her face away as if looking out the side window.

Jason looked at her for a few seconds before he started the car. He decided that whatever it was that was troubling her, she would tell him in her own way and in her own time. If she didn't tell him, then that would be her decision.

He started the car and pulled away from the curb. He drove down the street and turned onto College Avenue, heading south. Jason didn't say anything more as he drove toward his apartment. He tried to think about other things, possibly something that they could talk about that would help her relax. As he looked out the windshield of the car, he remembered that last night it had felt like it might snow. Looking around, he noticed that what little snow had fallen hadn't amounted to anything. It didn't seem like that was going to be anything to talk about.

"Is there any place you would like to go?" he sort of blurted out for a lack of anything better to say.

"No, not really," she replied in a soft quiet voice.

"I don't have much in the refrigerator for dinner, so I need to do a little shopping."

"Please, don't go to any trouble for me."

"It's no trouble. Even if you don't stay for dinner, I still have to go shopping, so it's no trouble. Would you like to go along, or would you prefer to rest at my place while I shop?"

"I think I would like to rest, if you don't mind. I didn't get very much sleep last night."

"I understand. I'll take you to my place and get you settled in. You can relax while I go get some groceries."

Jason glanced over at her again. She was still facing toward the side window.

Jason had stopped for a traffic light just as someone got out of a car parked at the curb. Kandace jump and jerked back away from the window at the sound of the other car's door closing. Jason realized that the two men who attacked her had done more than just make her frightened of their type, they had made her frightened of everyone and every little sound. Jason's temper grew hot over the thought that someone could do that to another person. He had seen it happen a hundred times, but for some reason it was different for him. It seemed more personal.

Jason turned off College Avenue onto Harmony Road. After going a short distance, he turned the car into the parking lot of his apartment complex. He parked the car in his reserved parking space and shut off the engine.

"Well, we're here," Jason said as he opened the car door.

Jason reached out and gently took Kandace by the hand as he helped her out of the car. Letting her take him by the arm, he guided her along the sidewalk to the main entrance.

"I live on the third floor, so you have a lot of stairs to climb."

"That's all right. I'm used to stairs. The only difference is I usually have Chester to get me started."

"Well, I'm not as well trained as Chester, but I think we can manage," he said with a chuckle.

The tone and the lightheartedness of his voice helped to relieve some of her fears. Her grip on his arm was firm, but not harsh as he guided her to the stairs.

"First step is six inches in front of you," he said.

She stepped up on the step and began the climb without any hesitation. Jason had to admire her ability and the confidence she showed as she moved up the stairs.

When they reached Jason's apartment, he stopped her at the door while he searched his pockets for the key. As he slipped the key in the lock, he wondered if he had remembered to pick up the place.

"I hope the place isn't too messy."

"I'm sure I won't notice."

The broad grin on her face helped him to realize what he had said. He felt a little embarrassed about forgetting that she was blind and wouldn't be able to see if his place was messy or not.

"I'm sorry."

"Don't be. It has been a long time since I've been with someone who hasn't fallen all over themselves feeling sorry for me. It's a nice change to have someone forget that I'm blind, even if it's only for a minute."

Jason opened the door and guided her into his apartment.

"I want you to feel that you can make yourself at home here," he said as he closed the door.

"I'd be careful moving around very fast. The coffee table has some very sharp edges," he suggested as he took her coat and hung it in the closet.

"Oh? I take it you've tripped over it a time or two."

"Well, as a matter of fact, just this morning," he replied as he threw his coat over the back of a chair.

He was feeling a little embarrassed again as he remembered the reason he had tripped over the table. He thought about telling her what he had done that caused him to fall over it, but decided that he would say nothing about it, at least for now.

"Is there anything you need, like the bathroom?" he asked not wanting to embarrass her.

"No, thank you. Just a place to sit down."

"Okay, we can manage that."

Jason took her arm and led her to the sofa. As soon as she sat down, he sat down beside her. She looked over at him and smiled.

"I thought you were going to the store?"

"Oh, sure. Will you be all right alone?"

"I would think so. I'll just take a nap, if you don't mind. I'm rather tired.

"Sure. Would you like an afghan?"

"That would be nice."

Jason got up from the sofa and left the room. While he was gone, Kandace slipped out of her shoes. After feeling the sofa to get an idea of where she was in relation to the arms of it, she stretched out, putting her head down on the large pillow-like arm.   Although she was in a strange place, she felt like she might be able to get a little rest there.

Jason returned with an afghan and laid it over her.

"There you go.   That should keep you warm," he said.

"Thank you for everything."

Jason smiled.   He knew that she could not see him, but felt that she knew.

"I'll leave you to rest while I go to the store.   If you need to use the phone to call anyone, it's on the end table above your head.   I'll be back in a little while."

"Okay."

"Oh, if the phone should ring, don't feel that you need to answer it.   Whoever it is will call back or leave a message on the answering machine."

"Okay."

Jason took his coat from the back of the chair and opened the door.   He glanced back at her before he left the apartment.

Kandace heard the door shut and the lock catch. The sound of the door being locked gave her mixed feelings.   It gave her a bit of a secure feeling knowing that the door was secure against anyone just walking in; yet at the same time, there was sort of an underlying feeling of being locked in, sort of trapped. It took her a few minutes to force herself to relax and feel comfortable. She was glad that Lieutenant Barrett, Jason, was concerned enough about her safety to lock the door.

She set her mind to thinking about Jason and all he had tried to do for her. She smiled to herself as she thought about how he had almost tripped over his tongue several times in his effort to make her feel welcome, and to try not to make a fool of himself.

She had spent a good deal of time last night before she drifted off to sleep wondering what Jason might look like. Now, she closed her eyes as she wondered what his apartment looked like. Was it decorated in modern, southwestern, or possibly contemporary? If the feel of the sofa she was lying on was any indication of the rest of the room, she was sure that it was a very comfortable place, whatever the decor.

She began to feel warm and untroubled under the afghan. For the first time since yesterday morning, she was able to relax and allow herself to drift off to sleep.

* * * *

As Jason pulled up in front of the store and parked his car, he realized that he had not asked Kandace what sort of things she liked to eat. He knew so little about her likes and dislikes.

He went into the store and grabbed a shopping cart. He began going up and down the aisles of the store, picking up an item here and an item there. As he walked along adding things to his cart, he tried to decide what to get for dinner. Thinking of her caused him to keep a steady picture of her in his mind.

The auburn color of her soft shoulder length hair and the deep green of her eyes, the smooth complexion of her skin dotted with a few small delicate freckles made him stop and smile to himself. He could remember the feel of her body as he held her while he waited for the ambulance to come to her aid. It was the last thought that disturbed him the most, that and the fact that someone was asking him to move.

"Excuse me, please," a rather irate looking woman said to him.

Although her words were polite enough, the look on her face and the tone of her voice were anything but polite. A quick glance around made it clear that he was standing in front of a display of eggs, and she obviously wanted him to move so she could get some.

"I'm sorry," he replied as he pushed his cart out of the woman's way.

The sudden interruption jogged him back to reality. He checked the items he had in his cart before he continued his shopping. After clearing the checkout stand, he returned to his car. He got into the car and started back to his apartment.

* * * *

"Chester!" Kandace screamed as her eyes suddenly flew open and she quickly sat straight up.

A cold chill came over her entire body. Her heart rate was very fast and her breathing was rapid and shallow as panic gripped her. In a state of near panic, she listened for a familiar sound, the ticking of her old clock, the dripping in her kitchen sink that Mr. Stockwell had not found time to fix yet, or the hum of her noisy refrigerator. She heard nothing familiar.

Slowly, the fog of sleep began to clear from her mind; and she began to realize that she must have had a nightmare. The smells of her surroundings, though not at all unpleasant, were unfamiliar to her. Even the faint sounds of the apartment were strange, as was the feel of the sofa.

It took her a moment to remember that she was not in her own apartment. As she slowly began to put things together, her breathing started to become more regular and she regained her composure. It was all coming back to her. She was in Jason's apartment, and he had gone to the store to do some shopping. Letting out a sigh of relief, she leaned back on the sofa and tipped her head back.

She took a couple of deep breaths. In her dream she had heard the voices of the two men who had robbed her and injured Chester. The whole frightening experience had been replayed in her mind while she slept. She knew that she would never forget the sound of their voices or the cries of pain from Chester when they beat him. Those sounds would most likely haunt her memory for as long as she lived.

As she regained her composure, Kandace remembered that it was Saturday. It was the one day of the week that most people liked, but it was the one day of the week Kandace dreaded the most. It was the same every Saturday. Her mother would call to see how she was getting along, then would try to talk her into giving up everything that she had worked for and return to Omaha where they could 'take care of her'. As much as Kandace hated to listen to the same tired old speech every Saturday, she could not let her mother worry simply because she didn't answer the phone or call her back.

Kandace remembered Jason had told her that his phone was on the end table. She could use his phone to retrieve any messages from her answering machine. Although she had no idea what time it was, she was sure that it was as good a time as any to check her answering machine.

Being as careful as possible not to knock anything off the end table, she reached out and found the phone. She dialed the number that would give her access to any messages on her answering machine and listened.

"Hi, little lady. Just lettin' yea know that we know where we can find you. Have a nice day." The message ended with a hideous laugh.

The sound of the man's voice sent a cold chill through her entire body causing her to drop the phone as if it were on fire. Panic clutched her chest and squeezed, taking her breath away. She wanted to scream, but no sound would come from her mouth. She fumbled around in an effort to find the phone so she could hang it up, as if hanging it up would make the fear she felt go away.

Just then she heard the sound of a key being placed in the lock. In a state of almost complete hysteria, she began to scream and tried to run to another room, but fell over the coffee table crashing to the floor.

As Jason fumbled with the key to his door, he heard the screams coming from his apartment. He dropped the grocery bags and drew his gun as he turned the key in the lock. Pushing the door open, he crashed into the room with his gun in his hand. A quick look around the room was all it took for him to realize that there was no one in the room, except Kandace.

"Kandace, it's me, Jason," he called out to her.

Seeing her on the floor in a state of panic, he stuffed his gun back in his belt as he rushed to her.

As he reached out to her and touched her, she began swinging her arms around in an effort to fight him off.

"Kandace! Kandace!" he yelled in an effort to get her attention and to get her to stop fighting him.

In the deep recesses of her mind, the sound of his voice penetrated her consciousness. Something deep inside her mind told her that she did not have to fight any more. She stopped swinging her arms around and tucked her arms in close to her chest as she covered her face with her hands.

"It's all right, I'm here," Jason said as he wrapped his arms around her and held her close.

Tears flowed from her eyes and heavy sobs jerked her body. As he held her, he gently rocked her back and forth in his effort to comfort her and ease her fears. Gradually, her heavy sobs subsided and she began to relax in his arms. He wanted to question her to find out what had happened, but not until she regained complete control of herself.

After several minutes of sitting on the floor with her in his arms, she was breathing more easily and she was no longer crying. He reached under her chin and gently lifted her face up. Taking a tissue from the box on the table, he gently wiped the tears away.

"Are you all right?" he asked as if talking to a small child, softly and quietly.

"Yes," she replied suddenly feeling embarrassed by her actions.

"Can you tell me what happened?"

"I called my answering machine. One of those men left a message on it."

"One of the men that attacked you last night?"

"Yes."

"What did he say?"

"I don't remember. I was too frightened."

"That's all right. I'll find out later.

"Come on," he said as he helped her to her feet. "You lay down here for a while."

Jason helped her back to the sofa. She did not resist, she simply lay down as he suggested and let him cover her with the afghan.

"You rest for awhile. I will be right here. I left the groceries just outside the door."

Kandace lay quietly and listened for every sound that Jason made as he retrieved the groceries from the hallway. Although she lay quietly and closed her eyes, she did not drop off to sleep again. She could hear him moving around in the kitchen as he put the groceries away. The noise he was making reassured her that she was not alone.

The sudden sound of the doorbell ringing startled Kandace, but she was able to get a grip on her emotions quickly knowing that Jason was there. She did not move, or say anything as she heard him walk across the room to the door and open it.

"Oh, hi, Mrs. Hamilton. What can I do for you?"

"I'm so sorry to disturb you, but I had a report of someone screaming in your apartment. I just wanted to be sure that there is nothing wrong?" she asked as she tried to look around him to see into his apartment.

"There is nothing wrong. Everything is all right."

"Is there someone on your sofa?"

"Yes, as a matter of fact there is.

"A woman?" she asked as if surprised.

"Yes, Mrs. Hamilton, a woman."

She looked up at him and a sheepish grin came over her face along with a twinkle in her eye. Jason wanted to laugh at her reaction, but decided that he would rather not get into any long lengthy discussion with her right now. After all, Kandace needed her rest.

"I hope that you won't mind too much if I don't invite you in to meet her right now. She is very tired and needs to get some rest."

"Mr. Barrett?"

"I'm only doing what you suggested this morning," he said with a wink.

She gave him a look that indicated she could not remember what she had said.

"Just this morning you told me to go out and find a nice girl, and that it was not healthy for me to live alone," he said with a big grin, then closed the door.

Kandace heard what he said and smiled to herself then closed her eyes. She was sure that Mrs. Hamilton had a shocked look on her face.

CHAPTER SEVEN

The afternoon passed rather slowly for Jason. He found himself checking on Kandace from time to time as she slept. He noticed that she did not seem to be resting very well. She was continually tossing and turning. Occasionally, she would mumble something, but he could not understand what she was saying.

Jason was in the kitchen making his favorite soup when she woke up. Kandace lay still on the sofa as she tried to mentally adjust to her surroundings. The smell of Jason's soup made her realize that she was hungry. The sound of him singing softly gave her a secure feeling that helped her to relax.

She stretched and yawned, feeling at least a little less tired than she had earlier. As she sat up, the afghan slid off her and fell onto the floor. Reaching down to retrieve it, she lost her balance and slipped off the sofa falling on her hands and knees.

Jason heard her fall and came running to her aid. He reached down, took her by the arms and helped her to her feet.

"Are you all right?" he asked, still showing the concern he had for her in his voice.

"Yes," she replied, a little embarrassed. "I just lost my balance when I bent over to pick up the afghan off the floor."

She looked up at him and Jason found himself looking into her beautiful green eyes. It's a shame that she can't see me, he thought. He let go of her arms and put his hands on her narrow waist. It was as if fate were drawing them together.

She must have realized it, too, as she slowly reached up and began to lightly touch his face, feeling every little line and wrinkle. Lightly her fingers moved over his nose, his eyes, his chin and his lips as her fingers helped her form a picture of him in her mind. She could tell that he was a handsome man, with strong features.

As her fingers slowly began to move along his hairline, he gently drew her closer to him. She tipped her head to one side and closed her eyes as her fingers moved through his dark wavy hair to the back of his head.

Jason could not help himself. He was drawn to her. He leaned down until his lips met hers. Her lips were warm and soft. He could feel her slowly melt in his arms as she lightly pressed her body against him. It had been a long time since he had held such a loving woman in his arms.

Kandace did not resist him. Instead, she let herself be drawn close to him, and let his lips meet hers. It had been a long time since she had allowed a man to hold her and kiss her.

Suddenly, he felt her body tense and she pushed back from him. As she pulled away, he wondered what he had done to cause the sudden change in her.

Kandace took her hands from behind his head, put them on his chest and pushed against him. She looked as if she was almost embarrassed by her show of affection. Her stern look of determination was soon replaced by a look of embarrassment.

"I'm sorry. I shouldn't have let you kiss me," she said flatly.

"Why?"

"Why what?"

"Why are you sorry? You are a beautiful woman. I don't know of a single man that wouldn't be proud to be seen with you."

"It's not fair."

"Not fair to who?"

"To you."

"To me! Now, that, I don't understand. If it's not fair to me, then why did I want to kiss you?"

"I'm sorry. I think the subject is better off dropped," she replied as she sat back down on the sofa.

"Fine," Jason said sharper than he had meant. "I'll have dinner ready soon."

Kandace heard him turn and walk out to the kitchen, but more importantly she heard the rejected tone of his voice. There was no doubt in her mind that she had hurt his feelings with her lame answers and poor excuses.

She reached up and put her fingers to her lips as she thought of his kiss. She could still feel the gentleness that his kiss had shown her, and the caring that showed in the way he held her. Why was she so set on preventing anyone from getting close, she asked herself.

Kandace had always told herself that she would never be a burden to anyone, no matter what. Ever since her last boyfriend could not deal with her blindness, she had used her blindness to keep those who wanted nothing more than to love her at a distance. Even though it made for a lonely lifestyle, it was easier than to risk getting hurt. It had become easier to do that than to feel the rejection of someone who could not deal with her blindness.

It had been years since anyone had kissed her like Jason had. She could still feel the warmth of it, and she could still feel how her body had responded to it. Yet, she knew in her mind that nothing could come of it. She was convinced that Jason would tire of her blindness, and that he would soon feel burdened by it. The more she thought about his kiss, the more she wanted to leave, to get away from him before it was too late; before she found herself involved with him.

Yet, at the same time, she wanted to stay. Was it possible that he was different? Was it possible that he would not see her as a blind woman, but simply as a woman? She knew that she was asking more than she had a right to, but if she left now she would never know if Jason was different.

She could hear him working in the kitchen. There was the sound of dishes being set down on a table and the sound of glasses clinking together as they were taken out of the cupboard. The one sound that was not there was Jason's singing. Maybe it was time for her to prove to him that she was not helpless.

She stood up. Slowly and carefully she worked her way to the door to the kitchen. On her way across the living room, she bumped into a table and a chair, but did not fall over them or knock anything over. She would have to get familiar with where things were if she was going to get around his apartment without running into everything. She stood in the doorway, holding onto the doorjamb.

"It smells good," she said making every effort to act as if nothing had happened between them. "What is it?"

Jason turned around to see her standing in the doorway. He had the feeling that he should apologize to her for speaking so sharply to her, but chose to simply try to forget it for now. Maybe he was moving too fast for her. If he tried to just slow down and show her that he cared about her and that her blindness was not a problem for him, it might go better between them.

"It's nothing special, just a very thick, very rich soup."

"It smells delicious. Is it time for dinner?"

"Pretty soon," he replied.

Jason glanced at her wrist and noticed that her watch was missing. He was sure that she had one when he held her while waiting for the ambulance.

"What happened to your watch?"

"Oh, I broke it. It must have happened when I fell."

"We'll have to see about getting it fixed. I'm sure you miss it."

"As a matter of fact, I do."

"If you're ready to eat, we can sit down."

"I'm ready," she replied as she stepped forward.

Almost instantly, Jason had hold of her arm. He gently guided her to the table and to a chair. As soon as she was seated, he stepped over to the stove and filled two bowls with the hearty soup. After setting them on the table, he sat down across from her.

"The crackers are dead ahead, the salt and pepper to the left of the crackers and a glass of milk at two o'clock. It's kind of a simple dinner so if you want something else, you'll have to ask."

"It will be fine, I'm sure," she said as she reached to the side of the bowl for her spoon.

She picked up the spoon, dipped it into the soup and carefully took a taste. The soup was hot, but not so hot that it would burn her. It was also as delicious as it smelled.

"This is good. Is it sort of a vegetable soup?" she asked.

"It's an old family recipe. It's really more of a beef and vegetable stew than a soup, but my family has always called it soup. It has some spices and herbs that my grandmother puts in. It gives it a little different flavor. Kind of an Italian flavor."

"Are you Italian?"

"Part Italian, mostly Heinz. You know, fifty-seven varieties."

Kandace laughed. It was the first time that Jason had seen her really smile, let alone laugh. He quickly noticed that she had a very pleasant smile, and the little wrinkles at the corners of her eyes seemed to add to her beauty. He also noticed that her eyes sparkled as she laughed. It struck him as a shame that such pretty eyes could not see.

The rest of their meal was eaten in relative quiet. It seemed to be enough that they were together and not getting too personal with each other. After dinner, Kandace sat at the table while Jason cleared away the dirty dishes.

"Can I help you with the dishes?" Kandace asked.

Jason knew it would be difficult for her to be of much help as she did not know her way around his kitchen.

"No, I can get it," he replied as he started running the water.

She was instantly sure that he felt she would be useless in his kitchen. Little did he know that she did most of her own cooking in her apartment, and she was about to tell him so when he added.

"I have a rule in my place. The first time you come here, you're a guest. After that, you have to fend for yourself and have to help clean up. You can wash next time."

She suddenly felt as if she may have misjudged him, but only time would tell. It seemed that every time she thought she had him figured out, he would surprise her. He was not like other men she had known, but was he different enough?

"I will hold you to that," she said.

"I just bet you will," he said as he turned toward her. "What do you say we go sit in the living room? We can watch a little television."

He immediately wished that he had chosen his words a little more carefully, but was relieved by her response.

"Sounds good to me," she replied.

Jason reached over and touched her arm. She stood up, took his arm and let him guide her into the living room. He guided her to the sofa where she sat down. Jason sat down beside her.

"What do you usually do in the evenings?" Jason asked.

"I read a great deal, and listen to the radio," she replied.

"Do you get out much?"

"No, not much. My job keeps me pretty busy.

"What is it you do?"

"I work in an office that develops computer programs for the blind."

"That must be interesting."

"I don't know how interesting it would be to a sighted person, but our programs do help the blind to be more independent."

Jason didn't know what else to say. He found himself just simply looking at her, and enjoying the fact that she was there talking with him.

"I thought we were going to watch television," Kandace said with a smile after what seemed to be a long period of silence.

"Oh, right."

Jason reached over and found his remote and pressed the button to turn on the television. The news had just ended and a commercial for Jeopardy came on the television.

"That's one of my favorite programs," Kandace said.

"Mine, too."

They spent the next half-hour watching the show and trying to give questions to all the answers read by the host. They laughed and guessed at some of the answers. Jason was pleased that they had found a common piece of ground where they could relax and be themselves.

When the program was over, they talked about it and decided that Kandace had known more answers than Jason. Jason didn't mind, he just enjoyed having someone to laugh and talk with. Sometimes his apartment became very lonely.

Suddenly, the ringing of the phone interrupted their discussion of Jeopardy. Jason reached over and picked up the receiver.

"Hello."

Jason listened as the person on the other end of the phone spoke to him. Kandace wondered what was going on, but decided that it was really none of her business.

"Are you sure that's one of them?" then he listened again.

"A picture won't do any good, she's blind. What we need is to find them and have her listen to their voices."

Kandace immediately knew that Jason was talking to someone who knew about the attack on her. She surmised that it was someone from the police department who was seeking identification of at least one of the men who had attacked her, but had not been able to locate him.

The realization that she would have to face her attackers, at least be close enough to them to hear them, sent a cold chill down her spine. In her mind, she could still smell the liquor on the one man's breath, hear their voices again and feel the fear that she felt when they hurt Chester. She felt cold inside and shivered.

Jason had glanced at her while talking on the phone. He noticed the little shiver and realized that just talking about her attackers was upsetting to her.

"Listen, Jeff, I'll talk to you in the morning. Get an APB out on Jackson, and keep looking for the name of the other guy. And keep me posted."

He listened for a few seconds more before hanging up the phone. He turned toward her and looked into her deep green eyes. He wanted to be able to tell her that it was all over, that she could go back to her apartment and feel safe again. But he knew better. She was not safe from them until they were behind bars, and it was his job to catch them and put them behind bars.

"Are you all right?" he asked as he reached out and touched her hand.

Her hand felt cold to his touch. As soon as his fingers touched her hand, she jerked away as if startled. He could sense that she was still frightened.

"I'm sorry. I didn't mean to frighten you."

"It's okay," she replied as she reached out to him. "I guess I'm still a little nervous."

"I can understand that," he said as he put his hand over hers.

She did not jerk away when he touched her the second time. His touch seemed to relieve her tension and help her to relax. Kandace simply sat on the sofa next to him and listened to the television.

Jason did not really watch much television. He was too distracted by the woman sitting next to him. He wondered what must have been going through her mind, but at least she was a little more relaxed than when they had first come there.

After awhile, Kandace yawned. She tried to hide it, but it was clear to Jason that she was very tired. He could not blame her. After all, it had been a long day for her.

"If you're tired and would like to lie down, you're welcome to use my bed. I'll sleep out here on the sofa," he quickly added.

"I don't want be any trouble."

"No trouble. I've spent a good many nights on this sofa."

"You do?"

"Yes. I sometime fall asleep on it."

"Oh. In that case I'll accept your offer."

"I'll give you the guided tour of the bedroom and bathroom so you can find your way around. If you would like to take a shower, you're more than welcome to do so."

"I would like that," she replied.

"Good. Let me show you around," he said as he stood up.

He reached down and took hold of her hand. She stood up and took his arm. He led her around his bedroom so that she would know where everything was located.

"Now the sheets are clean and there are two pillows if you want them."

"What about you?"

"I have an extra set of sheets, blankets and a pillow in the closet. This way to the bathroom."

He guided her into the bathroom. He showed her where all the fixtures were located, where the clean towels hung, and where the hooks were on the back of the door.

"I set your luggage on the dressing bench at the end of the bed. I'll close the bedroom door when I go out so you can have some privacy."

"Thank you. I really appreciate your hospitality."

"You're welcome. I guess that's about it. I'll leave you. If you need anything, just ask."

"I will," she assured him.

Jason let go of her hand and walked out of his bedroom shutting the door behind him. Kandace felt a bit relieved when she heard the door shut. She stood for a second where he left her to get her mind organized as to where everything was. As soon as she was sure of her position in the room, she went right to her luggage at the foot of the bed. It took her a few minutes of feeling around inside her luggage to find her nightgown.

Kandace was careful as she moved around the room. She did not want to stumble over anything. It was not difficult for her to find her way back to the bathroom. She had to do it every time she stayed in a strange place. It had become almost second nature for her to learn where furniture was located so she would not fall over it.

Once in the bathroom, she took off her clothes and hung them on the back of the door. Reaching past the shower curtain, she quickly found the faucets and turned on the shower. When the temperature was comfortable for her, she stepped into the shower. She stood under the water and let it run over her body. The warm water seemed to help her relax and soothed away the tension. Even the thought of being there alone with Jason no longer caused her concern.

As her thoughts turned to Jason, she could not forget the warm tenderness of his kiss. She touched her fingers to her lips as she tried to bring her image of him to her mind. She remembered the soft little lines around his eyes, the shape of his nose and the slight bump that indicated that he had broken it at one time. She could even remember the hard bristly feeling of several hours of growth of his beard. She was sure that he would have a thick heavy beard if he ever let it grow.

Suddenly, she realized that she had been standing in the shower for quite some time. She quickly lathered up with the fresh smelling soap Jason had left for her and rinsed off.

After shutting off the water, she stepped out of the shower and reached for the towel rack near the shower. At first, she could not find it and became a little nervous. Then she remembered it was on the other side of the shower. When she reached for it there, she found the large soft towel right where Jason had said it would be. With a sigh of relief, she dried herself then hung the towel back on the rack to dry.

After slipping into her nightgown, she carefully found her way back to the bedroom and to the bed. She pulled the covers down and crawled under them. Tucking them up around her shoulders, she closed her eyes and lay quietly. She listened for some indication as to what Jason might be doing in the other room. She could hear water running in one of the other rooms. She was sure that it was coming from the kitchen.

When Jason heard the water stop running, he went to the closet and retrieved the bedding. He made up the sofa for the night. Since he did not wish to disturb Kandace, he used the small bathroom off the utility room to get ready for bed. He could take a shower in the morning.

As soon as he was ready, he slipped out of his pants and shirt, then crawled in under the covers on the sofa. He lay for several minutes thinking about the woman in his bed in the next room. He could not get over how beautiful and independent she was, yet at the same time how very vulnerable she must be.

It did not take very long before Jason realized that he was very much interested in her. Not just as a victim of a crime or someone he was protecting, but as the very lovely woman that she was. He had to shake off his thoughts of her before he was able to drift off to sleep.

Kandace found herself thinking of Jason in ways that she had not thought of in a long time. She liked the way he treated her. Not as a blind person, but rather as just a person. She knew she had her limits, and she was sure that he knew it, too. But even so, she felt that he was not the type of man who would smother her and do things for her that she could do for herself.

She began to feel that she was really beginning to like him, and that was not good. Once he found out how much of a burden it could be to have any kind of a meaningful relationship with a blind person, he would not want to be around her. He would begin to feel sorry for her. It had happened that way before, she told herself, and it would happen again.

Tears came to her eyes as she thought about how things had turned out in her other relationships. She even had to scold herself for even thinking that Jason might have any interest in her, other than to simply help her get through the robbery and catch the men who did it. After all, that was his job.

It took her some time to get Jason out of her mind long enough to go to sleep, but sleep finally did come.

CHAPTER EIGHT

It was still very dark outside when Jason woke to a bizarre sound coming from his bedroom. It sounded to him as if a puppy was whimpering. It took a few seconds for the cloud of sleep to clear from his brain before he remembered that Kandace was sleeping in his bedroom.

Suddenly, there was a loud scream. Jason sat straight up on the sofa, threw off the covers and jumped to his feet. He ran into his bedroom and turned on the light. A quick look around the room revealed nothing, but one look at Kandace brought to light a very frightened woman. She was sitting up in his bed with her eyes wide open and staring off into space. Her hands were over her mouth and beads of sweat rolled down her face. She shook like a frightened child who had had a terrible nightmare.

"Kandace! It's all right," he said as he sat down on the edge of the bed.

"Oh God! I heard them," she cried out as she grabbed Jason by the arm.

"It's okay. You're safe with me," Jason said calmly.

Jason wrapped an arm around her and drew her close to him. As she buried her face in his shoulder, she wrapped her arms around him and hung onto him. He could feel her body trembling. He gently rubbed the back of her neck and shoulders while he whispered soft sounds of reassurance in her ear.

His efforts to calm her seemed to be working. Gradually, she began to regain control of herself. Her crying subsided and her breathing became more normal. As he continued to hold her close, he tried to understand what she was feeling and what she was going through. His anger at the two men who had done that to her grew quickly, but he could not let her know how angry it made him feel. That would just frighten her more and make matters worse.

He took his arms from around her and took hold of her by the shoulders. Holding her, he looked into her eyes.

"It's all right. You're safe here," he said calmly.

"I'm not safe anywhere from them," she sobbed.

"You are safe here with me. I will not let them hurt you again, ever."

"But...."

"I will not let them hurt you again," he repeated softly, yet firmly.

He looked into her eyes. Although she could not see him, he could see the doubt that remained in her eyes.

She slowly leaned forward and he guided her head to his shoulder. She felt a sense of well being come over her as she rested her head on his shoulder, and he once again wrapped her in his arms.

Jason could feel her body begin to relax as he held her. He could also feel the warmth of her body through the thin material of her nightgown. It was only then that he realized that he was wearing nothing but his undershorts. The feel of her soft, warm hands on his bare shoulders was just beginning to penetrate his consciousness. He wanted to lean down and kiss her, but it was not the time. He did not need a repeat of last evening.

"Are you feeling better?"

"Yes," she replied softly.

"You better try to get some sleep. I'll be in the next room if you need me," he said as he took hold of her by the shoulders and gently laid her back down on the bed.

As he laid her down, he could not help but notice her soft hair as it fanned out over the pillow. Her light blue nightgown with its deep V cut neckline gave him just a glimpse of her firm breasts, and the soft, smooth skin of her upper chest and neck.

Jason looked at her as he drew the covers up over her. He found himself thinking that she could be someone he could care very deeply about, or did he already care very deeply for her? The thought of trying to build a relationship with her passed through his mind, but what chance did he have with a woman who was determined not to get involved with anyone. Putting aside his thoughts, he turned and started to leave the room.

"Jason, please don't leave," she asked in a soft whisper.

Jason stopped and looked back at her. Although she could not see him, she was looking right at him. Her eyes, unable to see, still expressed her need for him to be near her.

"Are you sure you want me to stay?" Jason asked. He wanted to stay with her, but he also knew that it was probably better if he didn't.

"Yes," she replied with a slight quiver in her voice.

"Okay. I'll be right back," he said as he gave into her request.

He turned and went out to the living room where he retrieved his pants. After putting them on, along with a T-shirt, he returned to the bedroom with an afghan. He tucked the covers around her then laid down on the bed beside her, on top of the covers. He then covered himself with the afghan and laid there looking up at the ceiling.

He wondered what was going through her mind right now. It wasn't long before he realized that she had drifted off to sleep.

Sleep did not come so easily for him. He had a hard time getting Kandace off his mind. She was beautiful, yet she seemed so much in need of protection. She was afraid of just about everything, but then she had every right to be.

Jason's thoughts turned to the men who had attacked her. His mind suddenly became very busy shifting through what little information he had on her attackers. He had so little to go on. His best chance of identifying them was Kandace.

After what seemed like forever, he was able to drift off to sleep, but not without a great deal of effort.

* * * *

Jason woke when something moved beside him. He turned his head to find Kandace curled up next him. He took the quiet time to look at her. Her auburn hair looked as soft as kitten fur and was fanned out on his pillow. Her complexion was fair without a blemish except for a few very small delicate freckles. There was no doubt in his mind that she was one of the most beautiful women that he had ever known. She reminded him of a cat he had many years ago that was soft and warm, but very independent and headstrong when it suited him.

Kandace moved again, only this time she rolled up against Jason. The feel of him next to her alerted her senses. She immediately knew who was beside her, but she was a little surprised that he was still there.

As her thoughts turned to what had happened last night, she began to feel a little uncomfortable. However, it did make her feel a little more secure knowing that he had stayed with her all night.

"Good morning," Jason said softly.

"Good morning," she replied shyly as she rolled away from him.

"I wouldn't roll over too far. You might fall off the bed."

Kandace stopped and laid still. She didn't know what to say. It was a little strange having someone in bed with her. Usually it was Chester, but he always laid on the foot of her bed. He was definitely not Chester.

"If you will excuse me, I'll go use the bathroom, then fix us some breakfast," Jason said, thinking that it would be best if he got up before she was too embarrassed by him being in the same bed with her.

Jason did not wait for a response. He simply swung his legs off the side of the bed and stood up. He glanced down at Kandace as he left the room. When he was finished in the bathroom, he went out into the kitchen.

While he was working in the kitchen, he heard something fall in the bedroom. He stopped what he was doing and quickly went to the bedroom. When he got to the door, he reached out for the doorknob and started to open it, but hesitated.

"Are you all right?" he asked as he leaned close to the bedroom door.

"Yes. I just dropped something."

"Do you need any help?"

"No," she said sharply.

Jason stood silently looking at the door. The tone of her voice caused him to think of yesterday when she made it clear that she could handle everything by herself. It angered him a little to think of her that way. Everyone needs someone at some time, even sighted people.

He began to think that he might be overreacting to the tone of her voice. It made him stop and think about her. Maybe she wasn't dressed and didn't want him walking in on her. Maybe knocking something over was embarrassing to her, even though he had knocked over plenty of things in his life.

"I'll have breakfast ready in a few minutes," he said and went back to the kitchen without waiting for a response.

Jason had made coffee and was sitting at the table reading the morning paper when Kandace stepped into the doorway. He looked up at her. She was a good-looking woman, attractive in fact. Her shoulder length auburn hair framed her face and rested lightly on her shoulders. The sweatshirt she wore fit her well and gave her a casual, yet comfortable appearance. Her jeans clung to her body accenting the smooth lines of her hips.

"Jason? Are you here?"

The fact that she had to call for him brought back the reality of her blindness. He had been so consumed with looking at the beautiful woman in front of him that he forgot that she could not see him.

"Yes. I'm right here."

"The coffee smells good."

"I'll get you a cup," he replied.

"Thank you."

Jason got up and walked over to the counter. He watched her as she slowly moved into the kitchen until she found the table. Once she touched the back of one of the kitchen chairs, she sat down and rested her hands on the table.

"Here you go. It's hot."

Kandace reached out and Jason put the cup in her hands. She quickly found the handle and took hold of it. He sat back down at the table and watched her sip the hot coffee as he folded the paper.

"I didn't mean to interrupt you. Please feel free to read your paper."

"Nothing much going on. Would you like some breakfast?"

"That would be nice. Is there anything I can do to help?"

"I was just going to fix cheese and ham omelets."

"That sounds good, but I would still like to help."

"Well, ah, sure. If I direct you around the kitchen, do you think you could set the table?"

"I think so," she replied with a smile.

Something told her that he understood just how important it was to her to feel useful. He also understood that she was in unfamiliar territory and would need his help.

Jason watched her stand up, then directed her to the cupboard and told her what she would find there. As he prepared the omelets, he watched her lightly touch the different items in the cupboard until she found what she was looking for. With a little help in finding things from Jason, Kandace had the table set by the time Jason had finished preparing the omelets.

"Looks pretty good. I couldn't have set a nicer table," Jason said as he served her an omelet.

He suddenly realized that what he said might have sounded like he was praising a small child for a good job. He hesitated as he looked at her to see if he had hurt her feelings.

"Well, thank you," she said with a smile.

"I'm sorry. I didn't mean it to sound, well, ah..."

"That's all right. I think I did a pretty good job, myself."

Her comment relieved his anxiety. He served up his own omelet then sat down. He didn't want to say too much as he felt he had already put his foot in his mouth enough for one morning. He watched her as she ate. It seemed that she was deep in thought, maybe even worried about having to return to her apartment.

"I was wondering. I don't want to be pushy or anything, but would you mind too much if I helped you straighten up your apartment?"

Kandace stopped and looked up at him. He thought he could see a small tear in the corner of her eye. He wondered if she had been thinking about her dog, Chester, and was worried about him. There was also the strong possibility that she was afraid to return to her apartment.

"I know I have imposed on you quite a bit, but I would like that very much. I'm afraid to go back there alone," she admitted.

"I think we should finish up here, then go see how Chester is doing. After that, we can go to your apartment and clean it up. How's that sound?"

"Okay," she replied with a bit of forced enthusiasm.

Kandace was glad that Jason was willing to help her clean up her apartment, but she was still not sure that she could stay there. She was sure that Mr. Stockwell would have changed the lock, but that thought still did not make her feel safe.

After they finished breakfast, they cleaned up the kitchen together. Jason let her dry and stack the dishes on the table. When they were finished, he put them away. She thought about his comment last night about being a guest and smiled to herself. He had kept his word.

* * * *

As soon as they were ready, Jason drove Kandace to the veterinarian's office to see Chester. When they arrived, Jason guided her into the office. After a brief talk with the doctor, she was allowed to visit Chester.

Jason thought about letting her be alone with her dog for a few minutes, but she insisted that he come with her. When he first saw the dog, he noticed the dog was lying on its side. It looked like it was asleep, but Jason was sure that it was under heavy sedation.

"Tell me, how does he look?" Kandace asked impatiently.

"He looks like he's asleep. He has a large bandage wrapped around him, probably because of the kicking he got."

"Does he look like he's in pain?"

"No. I don't think he's in pain" Jason assured her.

"I want to touch him."

Jason guided her hand to the dog's large head. As her hand touched the dog, his eyes opened. He looked as if he wanted to raise his head, but couldn't.

Kandace lightly petted his head and gently rubbed his soft ears. Tears came to her eyes. She leaned down and kissed the dog on the head.

"Everything will be all right," she whispered to Chester.

The dog let out a faint whimper, then closed his eyes. Jason stood by and watched as Kandace petted the large animal again. He could see in Kandace's eyes the love she had for the dog, but that was understandable. After all, he had been her only companion since she moved there.

"I think we had better go and let Chester get some rest," Jason suggested softly.

He was reluctant to take her away from him, but they had other things to do.

Kandace bent down and kissed Chester on the head again, then reached out to Jason. Jason guided her hand to his arm, then led her out of the veterinarian clinic to the car. Once they were in the car, he drove to her apartment.

On the drive, she sat quietly facing straight ahead. Jason wanted her to know that he was there if she needed him. He reached out and touched her hand. She did not pull away. Instead, she turned her head to face him and smiled.

"I can take you to see Chester again later if you like."

"I'd like that. Thank you," she said.

Kandace lightly squeezed his hand. Her eyes drifted down as if she was looking at his hand. The feel of his hand helped give her the courage that she would need to face the task ahead.

As she sat next to him while he drove, she had time to think. Doubts began to fill her mind. She wondered how long it would be before he had enough of doing things for her. How long it would be before he got tired of taking her wherever she wanted or had to go? Why was he doing so much for her?

She let go of his hand and turned toward the window. Reaching up, she touched her lips as she remembered the feel of his lips against hers. She had liked the feel of his kiss and the way he held her, but she couldn't allow him to do it again. He would be like all the rest. He would not be able to accept her blindness and would soon tire of being with her, she thought. To let herself get involved with him was to allow him to break her heart. She wasn't sure that she could go through that again.

She felt the car slowing down and begin to turn. The car rolled over a speed bump, then turned and stopped. She was sure that she was just outside her apartment building.

"We're here."

Kandace looked toward him. She felt a cold chill run through her body. She wasn't sure she could return to her apartment.

Jason could see the fear on her face. He would have given anything not to put her through it, but it had to be done and the sooner the better.

"I'll be right beside you," he assured her.

Kandace took a deep breath and let out a long sigh. She was going to have to face the task, like it or not. There was no way out it. She took a deep breath, then turned her head toward Jason.

"I'm ready," she said reluctantly.

Jason got out of the car and walked around to her side of the car. After opening the door, he took her hand and guided her out. She took his arm as he led her into the apartment building and up to her apartment. As they approached the door, Jason noticed that a new lock had been installed in the door.

"The manager's put a new lock on the door. I'll have to go get a key from him. You want to wait here? I'll be just a minute," Jason asked, then patiently waited for her answer.

Kandace hesitated to answer him. She didn't want him to leave her alone for one second, but she was sure that he would think that she was being childish if she insisted on going with him. It was time for her to show her independence and to be brave. Besides, it would be for just a minute. She could stand to be alone for that long.

"I'll wait here," she said nervously.

"Are you sure?"

"Yes."

"I'll be right back."

She could hear Jason's footsteps as he walked back down the hall. As he turned at the stairs, the sound of his footsteps faded away until there was nothing but silence.

Kandace leaned against the wall. In her darkness, she could hear every little sound. She heard a door closing down the hall, the faint sound of music coming from inside one of the apartments and the sound of a phone ringing at some distant location. She had not realized how many sounds there were in the hall of the apartment building before. She had never just stood in the hall and listened. She felt so alone.

Suddenly, something brushed against her leg. She had not heard a sound from whatever it was, but it terrified her. With all that had happened to her over the past twenty-four hours or so, she panicked. She screamed as she kicked at it.

She heard the squeal of a cat as her foot hit the soft ball of fur against her leg. Realizing that it was just a cat that had rubbed up against her leg, she began to feel foolish. She had let her frayed nerves cause her to panic.

Kandace heard the sound of someone running up the stairs and turn into the hall. She was sure it must be Jason.

"What's wrong?" Jason demanded to know when a quick look up and down the hall revealed nothing.

"I'm sorry. I'm sorry," she said as she stood against the wall with her hands over her mouth.

Jason noticed that she was breathing hard and tears were rolling down her cheeks. Another quick look up and down the halls gave him no clue as to why she had screamed.

"It's all right," he said as he wrapped her in his arms and drew her close.

Kandace let him hold her. Being in his arms made her feel safe and secure. Resting her head on his chest and listening to the smooth even rhythm of his heartbeat helped relieve the tension.

As soon as she had regained some of her composure, Jason reached out and unlocked the door to her apartment. With his arm still around her shoulder, he gently guided her inside and shut the door behind them.

He held her while she rested her head against his shoulder. She began to realize how foolish she had been to panic over a cat. She leaned back and looked up at Jason as if she could see him.

"I'm sorry."

"It's okay."

Jason wanted to know what had caused her to panic, but he could see that she was embarrassed by it. If she didn't want to tell him, he would accept that. The important thing was that she was safe.

He looked over her head at the room. It was a quick reminder of why they were there, and why she panicked so easily. He let out a sigh at the task ahead of them, then looked down at her.

Kandace was still looking up at him. Her lips looked so inviting, but he remembered yesterday and her reaction to his kiss.

"I suppose we should get started," she said interrupting his thoughts.

"Yeah."

CHAPTER NINE

Kandace and Jason spent the morning cleaning up her apartment and trying to put things back in order. They started out working in the living room together. Kandace was having some difficulty dealing with her feelings. She would cry, then pull herself together, then cry again as she found her belongings scattered about the room.

Jason had seen the same reaction from other victims of similar kinds of crime. He tried to keep her mind off what had happened with questions about where things went and what did she want done with this and that. For the most part, he kept her from thinking about the two men who had invaded her life and turned her world upside down.

It was later in the morning when she went to work cleaning and picking up her bedroom. It was the room that she had the hardest time dealing with it. All she could think about was those two men going through her personal things, touching her most private belongings. She found it difficult to even touch her own clothes, knowing that they had rummaged through them.

Kandace stacked her clothes in piles on the floor to be taken to the cleaners. She had always done her own laundry, but this time she would take them out.

Once she had everything cleaned up, and her clothes ready to take to the cleaners, she sat down on the end of her bed as she had done so many times in the past. Automatically, she reached out to where Chester would lay while she got dressed to go to work, but he was not there for her to pet. Tears came to her eyes as she thought of him. She missed him, and wondered if he would ever be the same confident Seeing Eye Dog that he had always been for her.

Her thoughts were suddenly distracted by the sound of a vacuum cleaner running in the other room. She had been so deep in thought that she had almost forgotten that Jason was in the other room.

Kandace's musings turned to Jason. These past two days had been hard on her nerves, but Jason had made the terrible experience almost tolerable. He had been there for her when she needed him the most. He had been her guardian angel, watching over her.

She remembered yesterday afternoon when he kissed her. It would be a kiss that she would never forget as it warmed her heart and touched her soul. It had touched her more deeply than she expected.

She also recalled last night when he rushed to comfort her after her nightmare. Although she didn't realize it at the time, she could now remember how it felt to touch his bare chest and shoulders as he held her. She could also remember how it felt to have his arms around her.

Her thoughts and feelings were turning against her. She had tried so hard to keep men out of her life, but her mind was betraying her. Her mind was asking her to think about what it would be like to be held by Jason, to be kissed by him, and to be loved by him.

"I can't let it happen," she said out loud.

"What can't you let happen?" Jason asked as he stepped up to her bedroom door.

She had been so deep in thought that she had not heard the vacuum cleaner stop, nor had she heard Jason come to her bedroom door. His question had startled her.

"Ah....ah..."

"That's all right, I'm sorry I interrupted you."

"That's okay," she replied, relieved that he was not insisting on an answer.

"I was just wondering if you were ready to have me vacuum in here."

"Oh, sure. I'll just get these clothes out of the way."

Jason started to bend over to help her pick up her clothes, but stopped. It was her apartment and she knew her way around it. She was an independent woman and didn't need his help. Besides, she had already made it clear to him that she could do for herself.

As soon as she had her clothes up off the floor and on the foot of the bed, Jason turned on the vacuum cleaner. He watched her as she left the room. When she came back, she had a large cloth laundry bag. While he finished vacuuming, she stuffed her clothes in the bag and carried it out to the living room.

Jason was putting the vacuum cleaner in the closet when the phone rang. He looked at Kandace and saw her standing with hands over her mouth. He could see the fear on her face. He quickly moved to her side and put his arm around her.

"You don't have to answer it," he said softly. "Let the answering machine get it."

They waited until the answering machine answered the call. It turned out to be Kandace's mother calling. Kandace interrupted the answering machine to take the call.

While Kandace talked on the phone, Jason went out through the patio doors to the balcony. He leaned against the rail and looked out over the park across the street. At first, he didn't pay any attention to who was in the park. But as he began looking around, he noticed two men sitting on the ground leaning against a tree.

Jason found himself watching the men. Something seemed strange about the two men. He noticed that they seemed to be looking at the apartment building. He wondered what two vagrants would find so interesting about the apartment building.

Jason studied the two men from his vantage point. From the looks of them, it was not likely that they lived around there. It was then that he realized that they were watching the apartment, not the building.

They must have realized that he was watching them from Kandace's balcony. One of them pointed toward Jason, then they stood up and took off across the park.

Jason noticed that one of them turned around to see if he was still watching them. Jason watched them hurry off until they were out of sight. He thought about going after them, but did not want to leave Kandace alone. Besides, they were too far away for him to catch.

They had also been too far away for him to get a good description of their faces. They both had long gray coats on. One had a stocking cap that was orange and blue, while the other wore a winter cap with earflaps. The taller of the two men had a red scarf. They were wearing dark slacks and what looked like hiking boots, but it was hard to tell at that distance.

Although the sun was shining, it was a cold day. Jason went back inside and saw that Kandace was still on the phone. He sat down on the sofa and tried not to listen to Kandace's conversation.

"I'm doing fine, Mother. Everything is fine, really," she insisted.

It was clear to Jason that she must be having a hard time convincing her mother that everything was fine, but then everything was not fine.

"I'm sorry that I didn't get back to you, but it's been a hectic past few days," she said then listened.

"I stayed with a friend, last night," she explained then listened again.

"No, mother, I'm not coming home soon. Maybe when I can get some time off this spring."

"Yes. I promise."

"Okay. I'll call you next weekend."

"Love you, too. Bye."

Jason watched Kandace hang up the phone. She stood there looking off into space as if she were wishing that she had not lied to her mother.

Remembering that Jason was around, she turned and listened. When she didn't hear anything, she called out.

"Jason?"

"I'm right here," he replied.

"Oh, I thought you might have gone somewhere."

"No. I was just enjoying the view of the park from your balcony."

"Did you see anything interesting out there?" she asked as she walked toward him.

"No."

"Are we all done cleaning up?" she asked.

"I think so. Well, except for taking your clothes to the cleaners. What do you say we take your clothes to the cleaners on our way to get something to eat?"

"That sounds great. Will you give me a minute to freshen up?"

"Sure. May I use your phone?"

"Certainly."

Jason waited until Kandace had gone into the other room before picking up the phone. He dialed the precinct and waited for the phone to be answered.

"Homicide Division, Detective Walker."

"Jeff. This is Jason."

"What's up?"

"You know that mugging of the blind lady, Miss Clarke?"

"Yeah, sure."

"I'm at Miss Clarke's place now. While I was looking out toward the park from her balcony, I saw two men who looked like they were watching the place. When they saw me, they took off across the park in a hurry."

"What do you think you have?"

"A couple of suspects, maybe. One of them could be Jackson, but I'm not sure. I'll give you what I can on them. See what you can do to find them."

Jason gave Detective Walker as much of a description as he could of the two men. He knew it was not much to go on. It was a long shot that they were the men who mugged Kandace and injured her dog, but it was the best they had at the moment.

"Oh, Jeff, I want a rolling stakeout on Miss Clarke's apartment. We can't be too careful. If they are watching the place, she might still be in danger."

At that moment, Jason turned and saw Kandace standing in the doorway looking at him. From the look on her face, he realized that she had heard at least part of what he had said. He could see the fear in her eyes.

"I've got to go. Keep me posted on what you find out."

Jason did not wait for an answer from Jeff. He hung up the phone and walked over to Kandace.

"Do you think they are watching my apartment?"

Jason could hear the nervous quiver in her voice. He thought about simply reassuring her that there was nothing to worry about, but that was not true. He couldn't bring himself to lie to her.

"I don't know," he replied as he wrapped her in his arms. "I don't know."

Kandace leaned against him and let him hold her. She laid her head on his shoulder. The strength of his arms and the sound of his steady heartbeat seemed to soothe her nerves. She felt safe and protected as long as he held her.

Jason looked out into space as he held her to him. He wanted the two men who had turned her world upside down in the worst way. If they didn't catch them soon, she would live in fear for a very long time. She might never have the confidence to be on her own again.

"I think we need to find a place to have a nice quiet lunch. What do you say?" he asked.

Kandace lifted her head off his chest and looked up at him. She didn't really want him to let go of her. In his arms, she felt safe. In his arms, she felt protected.

Jason looked down at her face. Her beautiful green eyes seemed to beckon him. He took his hand from behind her and lightly touched her chin, lifting her face up. He looked down at her as he leaned down and kissed her soft warm lips.

Kandace did not resist. Instead, she let the warmth and gentleness of his kiss consume her. She allowed herself a moment of pleasure that she had refused to allow herself in the past.

It was a light kiss with all the tenderness that Jason could muster. It was intended to show her that he was not just a cop, but a man that cared very much for her.

As Jason drew back and looked down at her, he noticed that her eyes were closed. As he took his hand from her chin, she opened her eyes and laid her head back on his shoulder. She did not push him away.

Jason continued to hold her. His thoughts were of her. He wondered if she would ever let him into her life. He also wondered if his feelings for her might be caused by how helpless she seemed or by how much he really cared for her. He decided that it might be best if they just went someplace for lunch before he kissed her again. To kiss her again might be more than she was ready for, maybe more than he was ready for.

Kandace was also deep in thought. She wondered if she was falling in love with Jason, or if it was her need to be protected that drew her to him. Was he falling in love with her because he felt sorry for her and she needed him? What would happen to them when it was all over, and she didn't need his protection any more?

She was so confused. Should she let him into her life, or keep him at a distance like she had other men who had tried to get close to her. Keeping men out of her life had proven to be very lonely. On the other hand, the few men that she had tried to let into her life had not been able to cope with her blindness. Was Jason different?

"I think we should go get lunch," Jason said.

Kandace raised her head and looked up at him. She forced a smile.

"I think that would be a good idea."

She was a little relieved that she would not have to try to answer her own questions right now. It might be best to just wait and see if Jason was different.

Jason helped her with her coat, then led her out into the hall. After locking the door, he guided her down the steps and out to the parking lot. Once in the car, Jason looked over at her. She sat quietly facing forward.

"What would you like for lunch?"

"It doesn't matter."

"Okay, then how about Italian?"

"That would be fine."

"Great," he said, then started the car.

As Jason drove, Kandace sat quietly. He wondered if her silence had anything to do with him. She had made it clear the other day that she did not want to get involved with him. There was always the possibility that there was something else bothering her.

It wasn't long before Jason turned into the parking lot of The Olive Garden on College Avenue.

"The Olive Garden okay?"

"Fine," she replied.

Jason still had the feeling that something was wrong. She had said it was fine, but the tone of her voice and the lack of conversation during the drive didn't set well with him.

"Would you rather go someplace else?"

"No. This is fine, really."

As he got out of the car and walked around to the other side, he convinced himself that she was just worried about what she had overheard him say on the phone.

He helped her out of the car and guided her into the restaurant. The waiter seated them, then gave them the menus.

"Would you like me to order for you, or would you prefer that I read the menu to you," he asked not sure what he should do under the circumstances.

"You may order for me," she replied.

"Okay, but you eat at your own risk," he said in an effort to bring a smile to her face.

"Do you plan to order something really strange?" she asked seriously.

"No. I was just kidding."

The waiter came and brought them each a glass of water. After Jason ordered their meals, the waiter left.

"Jason?"

"Yes," he said as he looked up at her.

"Is there anyone around us?"

Jason looked around before answering. "No."

"Do you think they will come back to my apartment? I mean, do you think they will try to get in again?" she asked nervously.

He didn't want to frighten her, but he could not lie to her, either. He wanted to tell her what he really thought, but he felt he needed to soften it a little.

"I think that there is a possibility that they will come back, but it's not likely."

"Why do you say that? Did you see them outside my apartment?"

"I don't know."

"But you think it might have been them?"

"I don't know," he insisted.

"You're not telling me the truth," she said angrily.

Jason noticed that she raised her voice a little. He looked around in the hope that no one else had heard her.

"I'm not a child. I want to know the truth."

"Excuse me," the waitress said as she set a salad plate down in front of Kandace.

Jason noticed that the waitress seemed to be embarrassed, interrupting as she had. Kandace sat back in her chair and waited until the waitress was finished placing the bowl of salad on the table.

"Would you like some cheese on the salad," the waitress asked as she looked at Jason.

"No, thank you," Jason replied after waiting to see if Kandace was going to respond.

Jason waited until the waitress left before he turned back toward Kandace.

"When I say 'I don't know", it's because I don't know," he said quietly so that others nearby would not be able to hear him.

Kandace heard his firm steady voice and realized that she had made him angry at her unreasonable need for answers to her questions that no one could give her.

"If we knew who had done this, we would have a better idea of what to expect. But since we don't know who attacked you, and trashed your apartment, we don't have the slightest idea what they will do next," Jason said then sat back.

He suddenly realized that he had reacted to her fears much harsher than he had intended. He also realized that he should have been more sympathetic. She had been through a lot in a very short time.

"I'm sorry."

"I'm sorry, too. I know you are doing your best. It's just, just that, I'm..."

"Scared?"

"Yes," she admitted softly.

"That's nothing to be ashamed of. Let's eat. After we're done, we can go somewhere and talk."

"Okay," she agreed.

"Would you like some salad?"

"Yes, please."

They finished their lunch without much conversation other than Jason letting her know where things were located on her plate and on the table in front of her. What little was said was kept to casual conversation with little or no importance. Once they were finished, they agreed to go to Jason's apartment to talk. Kandace had made it clear that she did not want to go back to her own apartment, not just yet. Jason could not blame her for that.

CHAPTER TEN

Jason pulled into the parking lot of his apartment building. He helped Kandace out of the car and guided her up the stairs. Once inside, he hung up their coats, then guided her to the sofa.

"I'm going to tell you what we know so far," he said as he waited for her to sit down.

"We know that you were mugged by two men. They took your briefcase and purse, but dumped the briefcase when they found it too difficult to open."

"Wouldn't there be finger prints on the briefcase?"

"We're having it checked, but it is not likely that we will find anything. It was cold. They most likely wore gloves, plus it was handled by at least one other person, a bag lady. The chances of finding any usable fingerprints are slim at best."

"Oh. I didn't think of that," she admitted.

"We're sure that they did not dispose of your purse right away because they had time to think about robbing your apartment.

"We also believe that they are the same two men who robbed four other people over the past three months. We think that Chester may have saved your life by attacking one of them," Jason explained.

"Oh," she sighed as she tried to absorb what he was telling her.

Kandace wondered if Jason was keeping something from her. She had heard about several other muggings on the news, but did not realize that they were connected to hers. She also remembered hearing that a couple of the victims had died and at least one was in the hospital seriously hurt.

She wondered if Jason had been assigned to watch over her and protect her. If he was, it didn't really matter, she thought, she still liked being with him even if it was his duty.

As Kandace tried to absorb what Jason had told her, she realized that it did matter if Jason was assigned to protect her. It mattered very much. If that was the case, when it was over, she might never see him again. That thought added to her confusion. She needed time to find out if he was different from the other men, but how would she know if being with her was his job or his duty.

Jason noticed the strange look on her face. He almost wished he had not told her about the other robberies. He could not figure out what was going on in her head.

"Are you all right?" he asked.

"Yes," she replied, then turned toward him. "I just thought of something. We still have their voices on the tape in my answering machine."

"Damn, I forgot about that. Wait. Wouldn't they have been wiped off when you called and got your messages, or when your mother called?"

"No, I don't think so. I don't remember clearing the tape."

"I better go back to your apartment and get that tape. Do you want to come along?"

"I don't think so. I would like to rest if you don't mind?"

"I don't mind."

"The key's in my coat pocket," she said.

"Is there anything you need before I go?"

"No. I'll just rest here on the sofa."

"Okay," Jason said as he got up.

Jason took the key to Kandace's apartment from her coat pocket, then put it in his pocket. Just before he opened the door, he looked back and saw her lying down on the sofa.

"I should be back shortly."

"I'll probably be right here," she replied.

Jason was concerned about her, but he was sure that she would be all right in his apartment. He returned to his car and drove to her apartment.

Once inside her apartment, he played the tape to be sure that the voices of the two men were still on it. He quickly discovered why Kandace had panicked when she heard it. The threatening tone of their voices would be enough to scare a sighted person.

Just as he was about to leave, he stopped and looked toward the patio door. He wondered if the two men he had seen earlier might have returned to the park. He started toward the patio door, but stopped. He looked around, then went into the bedroom. Leaning up against the wall, he slowly pushed the curtain aside and peeked out at the edge of the window.

He scanned the nearby park. At first, he didn't see anything suspicious. He was about to give up and return to his apartment when he noticed a shadow move behind a large tree. He studied the tree and shadow carefully. Someone was behind that tree, someone in a long coat.

Jason dropped the curtain and ran out of the back of the building. As he moved around the end of the building, he stopped at the corner. From his vantage point, he could see someone in a long gray coat standing behind the tree. He could not see the person's face, but he was facing toward the apartment building.

A quick look around revealed a row of bushes that would hide his approach, at least until he was within a few feet of the suspect. Jason dashed off across the lawn and across the street to the bushes. He quickly moved along the bushes until he could see the tree and the man behind it clearly. He reached under his jacket, drew out his pistol and pointed it at the man.

"This is the police, put your hands in the air," he demanded.

The man did as he was told. He slowly raised his hands, then turned to look at Jason. When Jason saw his face, he knew that he was not one of the same men he had seen earlier. The man had a full beard with a lot of gray in it. Neither of the two men he saw earlier had beards.

"Who are you?"

It was clear that the man was frightened. His eyes were as big as saucers as he stared at Jason's gun.

"Joseph Willard," the man answered nervously. "Joey to my friends."

"What are you looking at over there?"

"Carl told me to watch that apartment building for him and he would give me five dollars."

"Carl who?"

"Just Carl. I don't know his last name. He told me I could have his coat if I would stand next to this tree and watch that building," Joey explained.

"Put your hands down," Jason said as he put his gun back in his belt.

It was clear that Carl had planted Joey to see if someone showed up. Jason wondered if Carl was Jackson's first name. If it was Jackson, he was probably not far away. He was probably watching to see if Joey was grabbed. Jason had fallen into the trap like a rookie, but Carl made one mistake.

Now Jason had someone who could identify him by sight, someone who could point him out in the police mug shots. If Carl and Jackson were one in the same person, he would know who he was looking for. If not, Carl would most likely be able to lead him to Jackson.

"Come on. You're going with me," Jason said as he took the man by the arm, turned him around and padded him down for weapons.

"Are you arresting me?"

"Sort of. I'm taking you to the police station. We're going to have a long talk and you're going to show me a picture of Carl."

"I can't do that, Carl will be mad at me."

"Carl will be mad? You have no idea how mad I can get. You don't have a choice. Come on," Jason said as he grabbed Joey by the hands and put handcuffs on him.

Jason led Joey across the street to his car. Once he had Joey in the car, he drove directly to the police station. When they arrived, Joey was taken to an interrogation room.

"You sit right there. I'll be back in a minute," Jason said as he pointed to a chair.

Joey sat down in the chair and watched as Jason left the room. As soon as Jason was gone, he began looking around the room. On one wall was a large mirror, but the rest of the walls were bare.

There were only three chairs in the room and a small table. It was very quiet in the room.

It seemed like forever to Joey before Jason returned. He set a cup of coffee down on the table in front of Joey, then removed the handcuffs. Jason sat down across from him.

"I've got a couple of people getting some books for you to look at. As soon as they get here I want you to look at them until you find a picture of Carl. You understand?"

"Yeah, but Carl won't like it."

"Don't you worry about Carl."

Just then an officer came in with two large books. He set them on the table in front of Joey and opened the first one to the first page.

Joey looked at the book, then up at Jason. As soon as he saw the police officer sit down at the table and cross his arms, Joey looked back at the book. He knew that he was not going to get out of there until he pointed out Carl in the mug books.

Jason stood by and watched as Joey began going through the book page by page. After a short time, Jason left the room, leaving the police officer to keep Joey company as well as motivated.

Jason went outside to talk to Jeff Walker. Jeff was working on a report when Jason approached his desk.

"Hi, Jason. How's it going?"

"I've got a guy in the interrogation room looking at mug shots. It seems one of our suspects is a guy by the name of Carl. I don't know if that's his real name, but I hope to find out soon."

"I put an APB out on the description of the men you called in, but haven't heard anything, yet."

"Don't hold your breath. This Jackson is a slippery guy. He put this bum in his coat and set him up as a decoy, and I fell for it."

"At least you have someone who could identify this Carl. If we're lucky, it might turn out to be Jackson. Look at it this way, at least we have more than we had," Walker reminded him.

"Yeah, but is it enough to help us find them? Kandace, ah, Miss Clarke is scared to death to return to her apartment."

"You can't hardly blame her, can you?"

"No, I guess not."

"I take it you have her hidden away some place?"

"Yeah."

"Where?"

"My place."

"Damn, Jason. If the old man finds out you have a victim hidden in your apartment, he'll have your hide."

"Where the hell else am I going to hide her?"

"In a safe house, with a policewoman," he replied as if it was the answer Jason should have known.

Jason got the drift of what Jeff was trying to tell him. It was not only a good idea not to get involved with the victim, it was one of the things that Jason's Captain insisted on.

"I've got to get going. Keep me posted if you find out anything."

"Yeah. You be careful," Walker said as Jason turned and left the police station.

* * * *

Kandace laid down on the sofa as Jason left. It felt good to hear the dead bolt on the door being locked from the outside.

Closing her eyes, her thoughts turned to Jason. She tried to visualize in her mind what her fingers felt when she had touched his face. She could see in her mind a handsome face with strong features.

As she thought about the two times Jason had kissed her, she touched her lips. In her head, she knew it was not a good idea to fall in love with him, but her heart was not in agreement. She was confused about what she should do. She knew that she should not let herself love him, it would only lead to disappointment. But she couldn't help herself.

Tears began to fill her eyes as she thought about the hopelessness of building a relationship with

Jason. She tried to shut him out of her mind, but that was proving to be difficult. She gradually drifted off into a restless sleep, one that kept her tossing and turning.

Suddenly, Kandace was awakened by a loud scream. In the fog of sleep, she didn't immediately realize that she was the one screaming. She sat up in an effort to catch her breath. She could feel her heart race. In the darkness of her life, she did not recognize the smells or sounds of where she was. It took her a second or two to remember that she was in Jason's apartment.

Suddenly, there was a loud knock on the door. She turned toward the door and held her breath. Then she heard a voice at the door.

"Jason? Jason? Is everything all right in there?"

It was a woman's voice that Kandace heard. She didn't know what to do.

"Lieutenant Barrett?" the woman called again, then waited for an answer.

Kandace took a deep breath as she tried to compose herself. She stood up and started slowly toward the door.

"You better open this door, or I'll call the police," the voice demanded.

Kandace followed the sound of the voice, reaching out in front of herself in the hope of not running into something. She let out a sigh of relief when her hand touched the door. Sliding her hand along the door to the dead bolt, she unlocked the door. She then slid her hand to the doorknob and turned it.

"Jason are you - - - -. Oh," Mrs. Hamilton said when she saw Kandace instead of Jason standing in the open door.

Kandace recognized Mrs. Hamilton's voice.

"I'm sorry, Mrs. Hamilton. I guess I was having a nightmare. I'm sorry that I disturbed you."

"Ah. . . that's all right, my dear. Please excuse me for asking, but who are you?"

"My name is Kandace Clarke. I'm a friend of Jason's."

"Oh. Where is Jason now?"

"I really don't know. Excuse me, but wouldn't it be better if we talk inside?"

"Certainly."

Mrs. Hamilton watched Kandace slowly turn around. She followed Kandace to the sofa and sat down next to her. Mrs. Hamilton sensed that something was different about Kandace, but couldn't put her finger on it. She looked normal enough, but her movements hinted that there was something very different about her.

"Are you all right, now?" Mrs. Hamilton asked, the concern in her voice was clear to Kandace.

"Yes. I am now. I'm sorry that I disturbed you."

"That's okay."

"I don't know when Lieutenant Barrett, Jason, will be back."

"Is there anything I can do for you?"

"No, I'm fine."

"Jason said you were here, but I guess you were sleeping when I came by and he didn't want to disturb you. How did you and Jason meet?"

Kandace wasn't sure what to say to the woman. Jason had told her that Mrs. Hamilton was nosey, but harmless.

"We met on the sidewalk a few blocks from my apartment," she replied, knowing that it was not a total lie, just not the whole truth, either.

"How long have you known each other?"

"Only a few days."

"Are the two..."

Mrs. Hamilton didn't get a chance to finish her question. The door to the apartment opened and Jason walked in. He wasn't sure how he felt seeing Kandace and Mrs. Hamilton sitting on the sofa.

"Well, Mrs. Hamilton. I see you have met Miss Clarke," he said with a grin.

"Yes. We've had a lovely talk."

"Oh, really? What brings you by?"

"I heard a scream coming from your apartment. I came to check it out."

"Oh," Jason said as he looked at Kandace as the grin faded from his face.

"Yes. It seems she was having a nightmare while resting on your sofa," Mrs. Hamilton said as she raised her eyebrow as she looked at Jason.

It didn't matter to Jason what Mrs. Hamilton thought, he was much more interested in Kandace. In fact, he was worried about her and her nightmares.

"I'm fine, Jason," Kandace said not wanting to worry him.

"I guess I'd better go. I look forward to seeing you again. I've told Jason that it is not good for him to live alone."

"Yes, I know," Kandace replied with a grin.

"Goodbye, Mrs. Hamilton," Jason said as he gently, but firmly led her to the door by the arm.

"Yes. Yes, of course," Mrs. Hamilton said as she looked at Jason.

Jason closed the door, then turned around to Kandace. He looked at her. She was so pretty, yet she was so easily frightened.

"Are you all right?"

"Yes. I'm fine. I just had another nightmare about those two men."

"Kandace?"

"Yes?"

"I don't think you should go back to your apartment unless we put a full time policewoman in your apartment with you."

"You saw something while you were at my apartment, didn't you?"

"Yes."

"I knew it."

"I caught a bum watching your apartment from the park."

"Is he one of them?"

"No. He's not one of the men that mugged you, but he knows who did. We know his name, but not what he looks like. I have the bum at the police station looking at mug shots. As soon as he identifies the man, we'll do what we can to find him and have him picked up. Then we will have you listen to him talk."

The thought that she would have to be close enough to one of her attackers that she could identify his voice frightened her. She could feel a cold chill go down her spine.

Jason could see her reaction. He sat down next to her, reached out and put his hand over her hand.

"Everything will be okay. I'll be with you. I won't let them hurt you again," he assured her as he gently squeezed her hand.

Kandace forced a smile and turned toward him. It felt wonderful to have him beside her, ready to protect her. She had always tried to be so independent, but right now she wanted, she needed a shoulder to lean on. Someone to be there for her.

"What do you say we have dinner and watch Jeopardy?"

She knew that Jason was just trying to take her mind off her attackers, but she didn't mind. She was feeling hungry. Not having to think about anything unpleasant would be nice.

Together they fixed dinner. She was still having a little difficulty finding things in his kitchen, but she was getting better at it. After dinner, they cleaned up the kitchen, then sat down to watch Jeopardy.

After awhile Jason noticed that Kandace seemed bored. He wondered what she normally did in the evening.

"You look bored. Is there something you would like to do?"

"I usually listen to the radio or read a book, but you don't have any books here that I can read."

"I could turn on the radio, or I could read to you."

He had said it without thinking. He wondered what she thought about his suggestion that he read to her.

"I haven't had any one read to me in a long time. There are so many books that I wish were in Braille. Some of them might be in Braille, but I don't have access to them right now."

"If you don't mind, I'd be glad to read to you. I have a lot of books. What would you like me to read?"

"You pick out something."

Jason picked out a Louis L'amour western that he had just started to read a few days ago. He looked at the cover, then at Kandace.

"How about a western?"

"Okay. I've never read a western," she said.

"Okay. Make yourself comfortable."

As he began to read, she settled in against him. By the time he had finished the first chapter, he found Kandace was asleep with her head resting on his shoulder.

He didn't want to disturb her, so he kept on reading out loud. After finishing a couple of chapters, he decided that it would be best if she slept in a bed. If she lay much longer against his shoulder, she might wake up with a stiff neck. As gently as possible, Jason woke her.

"I think it's time to go to bed," he suggested softly.

"I'm sorry. I didn't mean to fall asleep."

"That's okay."

"Maybe, I should go to bed," she agreed.

Jason stood up, reached down and took her by the hand. She stood up and smiled up at him.

"I think I can find my way," she said.

Jason got the feeling that she was exercising her independence. The tone of her voice indicated that she was feeling surer of herself and more comfortable with her surroundings.

"Okay, but if you need anything, just let me know."

"I will," she replied and squeezed his hand.

Jason let go of her hand and watched her as she worked her way around the furniture and into the bedroom. He was somewhat amazed at her ability to adapt to her surroundings so quickly.

It wasn't long before they were both ready for bed. Kandace called from the bedroom wishing Jason "Goodnight." Before long the apartment was quiet.

Jason lay on the sofa with his hands behind his head while he looked up at the ceiling. His thoughts turned to what his friend had told him. It was too late to tell him not to get involved with a victim of a crime. He was beginning to realize that he was falling in love with her.

Once again he wondered if she would let him into her life. He was certainly willing to let her into his.

Kandace lay quietly in Jason's bed. Her mind was reminding her of how good it felt to be held by a man. She had kept them away, but now she was beginning to feel very lonely. She wanted Jason to hold her. Not because she was scared, but because she wanted to feel the warmth of a man's arms around her. She wanted to feel loved, loved by Jason.

It wasn't long and she found herself off in dreamland. She was not having a nightmare, but rather a dream that refreshed her spirit and comforted her soul.

CHAPTER ELEVEN

As the sun crept in through the living room curtains, Jason rolled over on his back and looked up at the ceiling. His thoughts turned to the two men who had attacked Kandace. The thought of her attackers was never very far from his mind. There was no doubt in his mind that they would be caught. It was just a matter of how long it would take to find them and get them in jail.

His thoughts were suddenly disturbed by the sound of movement in his bedroom. He looked toward the bedroom and discovered that the bedroom door was open. He was sure that it had been closed last night.

He could see Kandace standing next to the bed with her back toward the door. Jason watched her as she pulled her nightgown up over her head and dropped it on the bed. He knew he shouldn't be watching her, but he couldn't help himself.

The smooth appearance of her skin, her narrow waist, the flare of her hips, the shapeliness of her buttock and her long legs would not let him look away. He watched her as she walked into the bathroom and shut the door.

It took him a minute or so after she disappeared into the bathroom to look away. He continued to admire her figure in his mind. As he did, he quickly came to the realization that he was sure that she did not know the door to his bedroom was open. He rolled off the sofa and walked over to the bedroom door. As quietly as possible, he closed the door. He hoped that she did not hear him close it, as he did not want her to think that he might have seen her naked.

Just as the door closed, the phone began to ring. Jason returned to the sofa, sat down and picked up the phone.

"Hello."

"Jason?"

"Yeah."

"Jeff here. We have a lead on the men who attacked Miss Clarke."

"Great. Have you picked them up?"

"No, not yet. We don't know where they are, but the one that the bum picked out in the mug shots is Carl Jackson, a petty thief."

"Not any more," Jason reminded him. "He's graduated to assault and robbery, maybe murder."

"Right. We're trying to get a lead on where he is. If we find him, we should be able to find the other one.

"Also, I got a strange call from a lady who said you promised her some money if she could find a purse for you. She didn't give me an address or her name, but said that you would know where to find her. Does that make any sense to you?"

"Sure does. She's a bag lady who hangs out in the area where Miss Clark was attacked. I promised to pay her if she found Miss Clarke's purse."

"Oh. Well, she said she found the purse you were looking for."

"Good. I'll stop and see her. Keep looking. If you find out where Jackson is hiding out, let me know."

"Will do," Jeff said then hung up the phone.

Jason set the receiver back on the phone, then looked up. He saw Kandace standing in the doorway to his bedroom looking toward him. He let his eyes drift over her. She was wearing a robe that looked very nice on her. He couldn't help admiring her.

"Good morning," he finally said.

"Good morning. Was the call about me?"

"Sort of. We have a lead on one of the men that attacked you."

"Oh. What was that about a purse?"

"It sounds like the bag lady that had your briefcase also found your purse."

"Are you going to go get it?"

"I thought I would as soon as I get a shower and get dressed."

"Can I go with you?"

"If you would like. Would you like to go by and visit Chester while we're out?"

"That would be nice. I'll get dressed."

Jason watched her turn around and shut the door to his bedroom. He got up and slipped into his pants. He hadn't even thought about the fact that he had been sitting on the sofa in his underwear. But than what difference would that make to Kandace, she couldn't see him. He waited for Kandace to get done in the bathroom, then went into his bedroom to get ready.

After Jason got cleaned up and dressed, they sat down in the kitchen and had a light breakfast. Jason found himself thinking about the woman sitting across the table from him. He wondered if anything would come from asking her for a date after her case was settled.

"What are you thinking about?" Kandace asked.

"What?"

"I asked, 'what are you thinking about?'"

"What makes you think I was thinking about anything?"

"You're very quiet this morning."

"Oh."

"Well?"

"I was thinking about the bag lady," he answered.

Jason wasn't really ready to tell her that he was thinking about her. He knew he should be thinking about her case and finding those responsible for what had happened to her and her dog. The bag lady was the first thing that came to his mind, but he suddenly found himself thinking about her.

"What about her?"

"I don't know. There's something different about her."

"What?"

"You have a lot of questions this morning. You must have slept well."

"Maybe I want to know what's going on in your mind."

"I sometimes wonder about that myself."

"Wonder about what?" she asked with a smile.

"About what's going on in my mind," he replied with a slight laugh.

Kandace laughed. The pleasant sound of her laughter and the sparkle in her eyes was a welcome change from the fear Jason had seen on her face so much over the past few days.

"I think we better get going."

"Okay," she said.

Together they cleared the table. Jason marveled at how quickly Kandace had adjusted to his apartment. It amazed him that she could remember where things went and where his furniture was located. She could already move around his apartment without stumbling over anything, as long as he left everything in the same place. There was no doubt in his mind that she was an amazing woman, and pretty, too.

After being helped with her coat, she took Jason's arm and let him guide her to his car. Once inside the car, they drove to the neighborhood where she had been attacked.

Jason turned the car into the alley at the point where Kandace had been attacked. He stopped the car and looked at Kandace. He noticed that the sparkle was gone from her eyes and that she had a serious look on her face.

"Are we there?" she asked as she turned her face toward him.

"Yes," he replied.

He watched her for a moment, then looked down the alley. Putting the car into gear, he slowly let it move down the alley toward the next street. He kept his eyes moving in the hope of seeing the bag lady. He was sure she would be in the area.

He glanced over at Kandace and noticed that she was facing directly ahead. She sat with her back rigid. She didn't move. He also noticed that she was breathing heavily. Coming back to where she was attacked must be hard on her, he thought.

"You don't have to be here. I can take you back to my apartment while I talk to the bag lady."

"No," she said more sharply than she had intended.

Jason looked at her. He wondered what must have been going through her mind. It was clear to him that she was frightened, but she was willing to face her fears and be there with him.

Kandace could not help herself. The thought of being there, where she had been attacked set her nerves on edge. If only I could see, she thought.

As the car reached the end of the block, Jason stopped again.

"What's the matter?" she asked, the tone of anxiousness was clearly heard in her voice.

"We're at the end of the block. We're going on across the street as soon as this car goes by."

"Oh," she replied, obviously embarrassed by her sudden outburst.

Once again the car moved forward. Kandace could feel the car as it dipped through the gutter on each side of the street. She knew that she was in the next block of the alley. She knew that they were moving very slowly.

"There she is," Jason said when he spotted the old lady pushing her cart across the alley at the end of the block.

Kandace could feel the car as it moved faster down the alley. The car suddenly stopped and she heard the door open. Her chest tightened as her fear of being left alone gripped her.

"Hold it right there," she heard Jason call out.

Kandace heard the squeaking of wheels stop. Then she heard them again, but they were coming closer.

"Is that the blind lady they stole the purse from?" the old lady asked as she looked in the car at Kandace

"Yes. Now where's the purse?"

"Don't get in a hurry, I have it here someplace," the old lady said as she started going through all the junk in her shopping cart.

Jason leaned against the fender of the car and glanced inside at Kandace. She looked nervous. It made him impatient to get what he came after and get her out of the neighborhood.

"Here it is," the old lady said as she held up the purse.

Jason looked at it. He had no way of knowing if it was her purse or not, but he was sure that Kandace would know just by the feel of it.

Jason reached for it. There was no need to worry about finger prints on it as it was a rough material which would not keep good clear fingerprints, at least not good enough to make a positive identification.

"Kandace, is this your purse?"

Jason placed the purse in her hand. She felt it. The texture was right and the snap felt like hers, but it was empty. She was used to it being full of her belonging.

"I think so," she answered.

Jason took the purse back and opened it. It was empty. There was not so much as a hairpin left in it.

"What was in it when you found it?" Jason demanded to know from the bag lady.

"There weren't nothin' in it," she insisted.

"I think there was. The two men would take her money, credit cards, keys and maybe any jewelry, but they wouldn't take lipstick, combs, the things only a woman would want. So what happened to it?"

The old lady glanced over at Kandace, then back at Jason. It was clear from the look on her face that he knew that she had finished cleaning out the purse.

"You said you was going to pay me for finding the purse. I found it. You didn't say nothin' about what was in it."

"Jason," Kandace called.

Jason looked at Kandace, then back at the bag lady.

"Don't go anywhere."

He leaned down and looked into the car.

"Yeah?"

"I don't care about what was in the purse. I don't even care about the purse. She can have that stuff. You're scaring her," Kandace whispered.

"I know. That's the point. If she thinks I'm going to arrest her and take her downtown, she might be a little more willing to give me what information she knows, and I'm sure she knows who Jackson is," he said in a whisper.

Jason straightened up, then turned back toward the bag lady. If she had heard any of the conversation between Kandace and him, she would not be willing to talk. There was no sense to continue that line of questioning in the hope that she would let something slip out. It was time to get to the point.

"Where does Carl Jackson live?" Jason asked bluntly.

"Who?"

"Carl Jackson. Don't play games with me. If I don't get the answers I want, you're going downtown. I've danced around enough with you long enough."

Jason didn't have to tell her what that would mean if he took her downtown. She knew how things were on the street.

"I don't know. He used to live a couple of blocks south of here, but I ain't seen him around for a few days."

"Where's he hang out when he has some money?"

"Over at Charlie's Bar, I think."

"You better be telling me the truth. If you're not, I'll be back," Jason said then turned and got in the car.

As Jason pulled away he looked back in the rearview mirror and saw the bag lady watching him. He wondered what was going on in her mind. He hadn't paid her for the purse and was sure that she was mad at him for that. But he also got the feeling that she not only knew the two men, but also knew where they were hiding. His gut feeling said that she was more a part of it than meets the eye, but there was no evidence to connect her to the muggers.

"Did you get any information from her?"

"Yeah," he said as he reached for the radio."

"Four Adam twenty-seven, dispatch."

"Dispatch, Four Adam twenty-seven."

"I need you to get hold of Detective Walker and tell him to meet me at my apartment as soon as possible."

"Roger. Dispatch out."

"What's that all about?" Kandace asked.

"We've got a lead on where we might find Carl Jackson. I want Detective Walker to meet with me and then we're going to check it out. You're going back to my apartment to wait."

Kandace had hoped to go see Chester. She was disappointed as she was looking forward to visiting her dog.

She also knew that Jason had to follow up on this lead before it got cold. Maybe, she could get him to take her to see Chester later.

As Jason drove back toward his apartment, he wondered what Kandace was thinking of him. He had been pretty hard on that old lady, but he didn't feel he had much choice.

"I hope you're not mad at me?"

"Why would I be mad at you?"

"You know. For being kind of hard on that old bag lady."

"No. I was thinking that she seems to know more than she is telling you."

"Yeah, I was thinking the same thing. It has been bothering me that she was able to find your briefcase so quickly after it was taken from you, but not your purse."

"You don't believe that she found it like she said, do you?"

"No. I think she had your purse that same night. I think she didn't expect to see me in the area that late at night and was moving it from where she had it stashed when I suddenly appeared. It was too hard for her to hide the briefcase in her shopping cart before I saw her, but your purse was much smaller. She probably had your purse hidden in the cart all the time."

"Do you think she was in on it with those two men?"

The tone of Kandace's voice gave Jason the feeling that she didn't think the old lady was in on it. Jason felt differently about it.

"I'm not sure, but I wouldn't be one bit surprised."

"Four Adam twenty-seven, Dispatch," the voice said over the radio.

"Four Adam twenty-seven," Jason replied.

"Detective Walker will meet you at your apartment in about 10 minutes. He's on his way now."

"Thank you."

Jason looked over at Kandace. She was facing forward as if she was looking out, but he could tell that she was deep in thought. He wondered what was on her mind.

"A penny for your thoughts," he said as he glanced over at her.

"Oh - - Ah - - I was just thinking about you," she said as she hesitated to go on.

"What about me?"

"I was just thinking about how dangerous being a policeman can be."

"Well, it certainly can be, but most of the time it's routine paper work and a lot of leg work. Say, you wouldn't happen to be just a little worried about me, would you?"

"I might be," she admitted quietly.

"Well, if I don't come back, you can have my apartment."

"That's not funny," she said as she looked toward him.

"I'm sorry. I didn't mean to make fun of it, but sometimes that's all we can do to keep our sanity."

"Oh. I hadn't thought of that."

The rest of the way to Jason apartment, they didn't talk. They were deep in thought. Jason didn't mind at all having someone around that cared enough to worry about him. It had been a very long time since anyone had worried about him.

Kandace didn't like Jason making fun of something as serious as what he did for a living, but she could understand. Sometimes it was the only thing a person could do to keep from giving up. She had done it herself.

When they arrived at Jason's apartment, he guided her upstairs. They had not been there more then a few minutes when the doorbell rang. Jason answered the door.

"Hi."

"Hi. Come on in," Jason said as he let Detective Walker in.

Walker looked around and saw Kandace sitting on the sofa. He noticed that she was a beautiful woman.

"Jeff, this is Miss Kandace Clarke. Kandace, this is Jeff Walker, a fellow detective."

"How do you do, Miss Clarke," Jeff said as he stuck out his hand.

Kandace reached out a hand. Jeff leaned forward and took hold of it.

"Nice to meet you, Detective Walker."

"Please, call me, Jeff.

"Okay, Jeff," she said with a smile as she let go of his hand.

"What's up, Jason. Dispatch told me to meet you here."

"I got a lead on one of the suspects. We're going to check it out."

"Okay. When do we leave?"

"Now. I'll meet you at the car.

Jeff took the hint that he was not wanted around while Jason said his goodbye to Kandace. He wondered how deep his long time friend had gotten involved with her. He didn't say anything, he simply went downstairs.

Jason watched his friend leave, then turned to Kandace.

"I shouldn't be gone very long. Will you be all right alone?"

"Of course. You will be careful, won't you?"

"I doubt that this guy will even be there. I think the bag lady was lying to me, but I have to check it out."

"I understand," Kandace said.

"When I get back, we'll go over and see Chester," Jason said in the hope of lifting her spirits.

"That would be nice."

"Okay, see you later."

Jason hesitated for a second, then turned to leave. Once outside the apartment, he locked the door. Jeff was waiting for him at the bottom of the stairs.

"Damn, Jason, you're playing with fire."

"What do you mean?" Jason asked as they walked toward the car.

"If the Captain finds out you have a victim living in your apartment, and a woman no less, you'll be lucky if you end up walking a beat."

"Right now, you're the only one who knows."

"I'm sure as hell not going to say anything, but how long do you think you can keep it a secret?"

"Until we catch the bad guys. Now get in the car," Jason said impatiently.

Jason got in one side, while Jeff got in the other. Jason took a look up at his apartment before he drove away. On the drive toward Charlie's Bar, Jason explained the situation to Jeff.

CHAPTER TWELVE

Kandace sat on the sofa, her mind going a mile a minute. All she could think about was Jason and the danger he might be walking into by going to that bar in search of one of her attackers. A cold shiver went through her as she thought about him and the possibility that he might get hurt. She could think of nothing else.

She suddenly realized that Jason had become very important to her, and that he meant something to her that she might never have again. She was beginning to understand that in spite of her efforts not to fall in love with anyone, she had fallen in love with him.

In just the few days that they had known each other, he had brought her out of her protective shell and into the real world. He had brought her back to life. Back to a life that was full of surprises and uncertainties, but wasn't that what made a person feel alive?

She tipped her head back and closed her eyes. She began to wonder if she was the only one of them that felt that way. If Jason didn't share her feelings, she knew that she was in for a long lonely time. But she also realized that she had to take the chance that he did feel the same way about her. If her life was going to amount to anything more than the routine of her work and the loneliness of being alone, she had to let someone into her life. Jason was that someone she wanted in her life.

In her mind, she could still feel the warmth of his kiss, the tenderness of his lips against hers and the strength of his arms around her. Just remembering how it felt to have him hold her in his arms was enough to assure her that he cared for her, too. At least that thought was enough for now.

* * * *

"Here it is," Jason said as he stopped the car in front of Charlie's Bar.

Jeff and Jason got out of the car and looked around. The bar was located in an older and one of the less desirable neighborhoods of the city. Only in recent years had the people in the area begun to clean it up and try to make it a safe neighborhood again, but Charlie's Bar remained the same.

Charlie's Bar was a bit of an eyesore. It was also a well-known hangout for the undesirables like drug pushers and thugs. It was frequented by the police due to complaints of harassment of local people and to break up fights. It was the scene of several drug arrests in just the past few months.

Jeff looked over the car at Jason. He nodded that it was time. He waited for Jason to join him on the sidewalk, and then they walked into the bar.

The inside of the bar was as dreary as the outside, only darker. The windows had been covered up with advertisements. There were a few old lighted signs that advertised different kinds of beer. The old wooden bar had several stools lined up in front of it, most of them with torn or cut covers. The tables scattered around the room were old and not in very good shape. The few booths along one wall were not in any better condition.

Jeff and Jason stood near the door until their eyes adjusted to the dimly lit room. They took a minute to look around to see who was there. It was pretty quiet at that time of day with only a couple of patrons.

Over in one corner was a fat lady in a Muumuu dress sipping on a beer. She had curlers in her hair and looked as if she didn't care about much of anything.

Down at the end of the bar was a man with a beard and long hair. He looked like he hadn't had a bath in a month and had no idea what a comb was. His coat was old and worn as were the beat up old tennis shoes he wore. He sat at the bar and stared at the full glass of beer in front of him. Jason was sure that he had come into the bar more to get out of the cold than to have a beer. He didn't even look up to see who had come in. He just sat there and stared at the glass of beer as if trying to decide if he should drink it or not.

Behind the bar was a large man wearing a gray shirt with the sleeves rolled up. He had a dingy white apron tied around his more than ample waist. He was wiping a glass while he chewed on the end of a big black cigar.

"You gents want somethin'?"

Jason walked up to the bar while Jeff leaned against the wall near the door.

"Yeah. We're looking for Carl Jackson. You know where he is?"

"What you want him for? He owe you money?" the bartender said with a sarcastic chuckle.

"You might say that."

"It figures. A guy comes into a little money and everyone is out to take it away from him."

"When did he come into any money?"

"A couple of days ago, I guess."

"When did you see him last?"

"Now I'm not going to tell you that. If you want him, you're going to have to find him yourself," the bartender said with a grin.

Jason took a slow look around the bar, then turned back to the bartender. He reached in his pocket and pulled out his badge and ID.

"I'm Lieutenant Barrett, and that is Detective Walker. Do you want to rethink that answer, or would you like your bar closed down by the Health Department as a health hazard?"

The bartender looked at the badge, then at Jason. The grin in the bartender's face disappeared rather quickly. He glanced over Jason's shoulder at Jeff who was still standing at the door.

Just as the bartender was about to say something a door near the end of the bar opened. A man wearing an old sweater and dark pants stepped out of the back room. The man looked as if he had just gotten out of bed.

"Hey, man, you got any - - -," his voice faded quickly when he saw Jason at the bar.

As Jason turned and looked at the man, the man quickly turned around and ran back through the door.

"Jeff," Jason yelled as he took off after the man.

Jason crashed through the door and on into the storage room with Jeff hot on his heels. The back door of the bar was open and Jason charged through it. Once outside, Jason stopped and took a quick look around. He caught a glimpse of someone darting around the corner, and took off after the man again.

The man ran across the street and into an alley. Jason pursued the man down the alley. He was slowly gaining on him when the man turned and jumped a fence into a yard. By the time Jason got to the fence, the man was nowhere in sight. A quick look around was all it took for Jason to realize that he had lost him. There was any number of places inside that yard he could hide, or simply disappear onto another street.

"Damn," Jason said as he hit a fence post in frustration.

Jason turned around in time to see Jeff bringing the car down the alley toward him. He leaned against the fence to catch his breath while he waited for Jeff to pull up beside him.

When Jeff stopped, Jason opened the door and got in the car.

"I lost him."

"Where to now?"

"Back to the bar."

Jeff drove on around the block and went back to the bar. When they arrived at the bar, they got out. Jason was the first one through the front door. He walked up to the bar while Jeff stopped and stood next to the door.

"That was Jackson, wasn't it?"

"Yeah, and you couldn't even catch him," the bartender said with a slight chuckle.

"I'm going to say this just once, so you better listen up. Where has Jackson been staying?"

"You had your chance at him, and you blew it," the bartender said with a grin.

Jason looked at the bartender. He could see that this man was not going to cooperate with him without some incentive. It dawned on Jason that Jackson did not have a coat on when he chased him out the back door. It was too cold to be outside without a coat. He looked toward the door that

Jackson had used to enter the bar. Jason remembered that right after Jackson and his friend had attacked Kandace, they suddenly disappeared. They had to be holding up some place, and maybe that place was there.

Jason slowly backed away from the bar and walked toward the door. As he reached for the doorknob, he glanced back at the bartender. There was no smile on the bartender's face now. In fact, he looked a little worried.

"Jeff, keep an eye on him. If he so much as moves, put him down," Jason said, his voice showing that he was not going to tolerate any argument.

Jeff didn't hesitate. He stepped up closer to the bar and slid his hand inside his coat. The bartender backed up against the back of the bar and stood quietly.

Jason went into the back room and began looking around. At first all he found were cases of beer and beer kegs, a few boxes of bar supplies and paper towels. But when he got to the back of the room, he found a cot and a crate that was being used as a nightstand behind a stack of boxes. On the stand were a small radio, a small table lamp and a pink wallet.

At first, Jason thought that it was the place where the bartender would come to rest, but the pink wallet made him think again. It was the same color, and looked to be made of the same material as Kandace's purse. He was now sure that it was where Jackson had been hiding out.

Jason didn't touch anything. He returned to the bar.

"What's your name?" Jason asked.

"McDonnally, James McDonnally," he replied sharply.

"Well, Mr. McDonnally, you are under arrest for harboring a felon," Jason said as he pulled his gun out from under his coat.

"Come out from behind the bar with your hands up," Jeff said as he drew his gun.

McDonnally did as he was told. As soon as McDonnally was out from behind the bar, Jason began reading him his rights while Jeff put handcuffs on him. After he was cuffed, Jeff led him to a table and sat him down. Jason sat across from him.

"We need to clear the bar," Jason said as he looked up at Jeff.

"Okay, everybody out. This place is closed," Jeff ordered.

The two patrons looked a little disgusted. The man at the bar looked at Jeff and then at the beer. He wasn't very happy about leaving, but he left. As soon as they were out, Jeff closed and locked the door.

Jeff walked back to the table. He stood behind McDonnally.

"What did you find?"

"I found a bed and night stand in the back corner of the storage room. Miss Clarke's wallet is on the night stand," Jason said without taking his eyes off McDonnally.

"You need to call it in. I want the lab people out here to go over this place."

"You can't do that without a search warrant," McDonnally objected.

"Yes I can. You are going to be charged with harboring a felon. That should put you away for several years. By the way, do you want a lawyer, or will you answer my questions."

"I want a lawyer," McDonnally insisted.

"Okay, but he better be a good one because we have you cold."

"I'll be right back," Jeff said. "I'll go call it in."

"I want a lawyer, now."

"You'll get a lawyer before any questions are asked. Right now, you just sit there and be quiet."

Within a few minutes Jeff returned.

"I called for the lab people to come down and go over the place. I also called for a unit to come and take McDonnally in for booking."

"Great. Watch him for a minute while I look around," Jason said as he stood up.

Jeff sat down at the table to keep an eye on McDonnally. Jason walked behind the bar and began looking around. Under the bar, he found a club that looked like it would make a pretty lethal weapon.

He turned around and looked along the back of the bar. He noticed something that looked like it might be a credit card half-hidden under some napkins and receipts. Not wanting to touch anything until the lab people were finished, he took a pencil from his pocket and pushed the napkins aside. He then worked the credit card out on the counter where he could see it.

"Well, well. What do we have here? Looks like a credit card that belongs to Miss Kandace Clarke. I wonder how that got here."

"She left it here the other night. I was keeping it until she came back," McDonnally said.

"Oh really?"

"Yeah."

"And how did she get here?"

"What?" he asked confused by his question.

"I asked how did she get here?"

"Drove, I guess. How would I know? She came in, ordered a beer and sat down and drank it. In fact, she had several beers."

"Where was her dog?" Jason asked.

"I don't know what you're talking about. She didn't have no dog. She came in, pointed out the kind of beer she wanted and I served it to her. That's all."

Jason looked at McDonnally. He wondered if he was just plain lying or if someone else had come into the bar with Miss Clarke's credit card. The look on McDonnally face gave him no clue to the answer.

"Did Miss Clarke pay for her drinks with the credit card?"

"Yeah, sure. How the hell do you think I got it?"

"Then you have a signed receipt, don't you?"

"Yeah, I guess. It's under the tray in the cash register."

"Mind if I look?"

"Yeah, I mind. Say, what's this all about?"

"Miss Clarke could not drive to your bar. She is blind and has a Seeing Eye dog, which your friend Carl Jackson injured when he robbed Miss Clarke of her purse and briefcase."

"You're not going to pin that on me. I had nothing to do with it. A woman left that credit card. She said she was Kandace Clarke."

It was clear that McDonnally was afraid that he was going to end up being charged with robbery as well as harboring a felon. The sweat started to roll down the sides of the fat man's face. He felt he was between a rock and a hard place. If he told them about Jackson, Jackson would kill him. If he didn't tell them, he was probably going to jail for a long time.

"I think you need a lawyer," Jason commented.

Jason watched McDonnally sweat. He was twitching and turning in the chair and his eyes moved quickly from side to side. There was no doubt in Jason's mind that McDonnally was scared.

Just then they heard the door rattle followed by a firm knock on the door. Jeff stood up and went to the door. Two uniformed officers were standing outside.

"Come on in."

"We understand you have someone you want transported."

"Yeah. Take Mr. McDonnally downtown and book him for harboring a felon. We'll be down in a little while to do the paperwork. Make sure he gets a chance to call a lawyer. He's going to need one," Jason explained.

"Will do," the officer said as he stepped up close to McDonnally.

"We gave him his rights," Jeff added as the two officers escorted McDonnally out of the bar.

Once McDonnally was out of the bar, Jason and Jeff started looking around. Jason went through a bunch of papers under the tray in the cash register, careful not to touch anything with his fingers. As he sorted through the papers with his pencil, he found a credit card slip that had been signed

'Kandace R. Clark'. He immediately noticed that the "e" had been left off the last name, and that the handwriting appeared strained. He flipped the credit card over on the counter and looked at the signature on the back. It was obvious that it was not Kandace's signature.

Jeff had gone to the back room to look around. As he looked around the area surrounding the crate that was used as a nightstand, he noticed something on the floor between the crate and the cot. It was a crumpled up piece of paper. He bent down and picked it up. He straightened out the small piece of paper and discovered a telephone number.

"Jason," he called out as he looked at the number.

"Yeah?" Jason said as he came into the storage room.

"Look here," he said as he held out the paper for Jason to see. "Looks like a cell phone number. I wonder whose it is?"

"I don't know," Jason replied. "I think we should find out. It could lead us to Carl Jackson or his partner."

"I'll get on it," Jeff replied.

Jason stood in the storage room as Jeff went out to the car. He stood looking at the wall, but it was not the wall that he was thinking about. It was time to find out what the woman looked like that had used Kandace's credit card. The only one who knew what she would look like was McDonnally.

Jason's thoughts were interrupted by the sound of people entering the bar. He left the storage room and returned to the bar. He quickly found that the lab people had arrived and an old friend of his was with them.

"Hi, Mack. How's it going?"

"Not bad, Jason. What's going on here? Are we looking for anything special?"

"Yeah. Fingerprints on the credit card next to the cash register would certainly be nice. You have your job cut out for you."

"What you working on?"

"I'm working on the mugging of that blind lady. The one where the thugs almost killed her Seeing Eye dog. We think it's connected to the other muggings where the victims weren't so lucky."

"Yeah. I heard about that. What's this world coming to with low life that would do a thing like that? I understand this lady is your only witness."

"Yeah.

"I suppose they thought she would be an easy target, she couldn't identify them in a lineup. But they forgot one thing, she can identify them by the sound of their voices.

"Yes, she can. Her dog may very well have saved her life when he attacked one of them. It almost cost the dog his life," Jason added.

"That's a shame. I'll see what I can find for you."

"Thanks, Mack."

Jason went out to the car. He saw Jeff leaning against the car talking on the police radio. As he approached, Jeff put the mike down.

"That phone number belongs to a Mildred Moffett. It gives the home address as 22317 Horsetooth Road with a post office box for billing. I've got a car going out to check on the address," Jeff explained.

"I didn't think there were any houses out that far on Horsetooth Road."

"I don't think there is, but I'm having it checked out."

"Good. Let's go back to the office. I want to call Kandace and make sure everything is okay. Then let's have a little discussion with McDonnally."

CHAPTER THIRTEEN

When Jason and Jeff returned to the police station, Jeff went to the jail to retrieve McDonnally while Jason went to his desk and called Kandace. The phone rang only twice before it was picked up.

"Hi. It's me," Jason said.

"Hi, me," Kandace replied, the tone of her voice indicating that she was glad to hear him.

"How are you doing?"

"I'm doing fine. Your landlady stopped by, but I didn't answer the door."

"That's fine. I was a little afraid that you wouldn't answer the phone."

"It did make me a little nervous, but I thought I better answer it just in case it was you."

Jason thought he could hear a slight tone of pleasure in her voice, hopefully because he had taken the time to call her. He was glad that she was not so frightened that she would not answer the phone.

"How did things go at the bar? Did you find out anything?"

"We sure did. I found one of your credit cards. It seems some lady used it to buy beer."

"I hope she enjoyed the beer," Kandace said with a chuckle.

"I hope so, too. I need to ask you a question. Did you hear the sound of a woman's voice, or maybe get a hint of the smell of perfume, or anything that might make you think that there was a woman somewhere close when you were attacked?"

"No, not that I can remember," she replied after giving it a moment's thought. "Just the two men I told you about."

"Not even in the distance?"

"No, I don't think so. Why? Is it important?"

"I don't know. I have this gut feeling that there's a woman behind this, or at least that a woman took part in it in some way," Jason said.

"Oh. Is that what you found out at the bar?"

"No, not really. We found out that Carl Jackson was holding up there, but we still don't know where the other guy is. The bartender was hiding Jackson in his back room. We arrested the bartender in the hope of finding out more, but I don't know how much help he will be.

"It may be a while before I get home. Will you be all right?"

"Sure. I'll wait dinner until you get home."

"Thanks. I'll see you later," Jason said as he hung up.

He stood for a second looking at the phone. He liked the sound of her voice and the fact that she would wait dinner until he got 'home'. It made him wonder what it would be like if it was for real. It also made him wonder if she was cooking dinner and if so what she might be making.

"I've got McDonnally in one of the interrogation rooms whenever you're ready," Jeff said disturbing Jason's thoughts.

"I'm coming right now."

Jason followed Jeff down the hall to the interrogation room. Once inside, he sat down at the table across from McDonnally. Jason took a quick look around the room. The only other person in the room was Jeff.

"Where's your lawyer?" Jason asked.

"Are you formally charging me with anything?"

"Not yet," Jason said cautiously as he wondered why McDonnally had a sudden change of heart.

"If I cooperate with you, what will I get in exchange?"

"That's going to depend on what we get from you, and how cooperative you are in giving it to us."

McDonnally looked at Jason. He wasn't sure if he should try to bargain with him, or if it would be in his best interest to tell them what they wanted to know and hope for the best. Jason interrupted his thoughts.

"I won't make any promises, but the more you do for us, the more we're likely to do for you.

That's the best deal you're going to get, take it or leave it."

McDonnally sat there looking at Jason, trying to decide if he meant what he said. He didn't know Lieutenant Barrett, but he had heard of him. He had a reputation for being a hard man, but a fair one. Maybe if he helped, Jason would go lighter on him. He was pretty sure that if he didn't cooperate, Jason would do everything he could to make it tough on him.

Jason waited to see what McDonnally was going to do. He could see that McDonnally was hashing it over in his mind. McDonnally had already said that he wanted a lawyer. If he questioned him before he rescinded that request, nothing he said could be used against him in a court of law. Jason was growing impatient.

"Take him back to a cell until he can get a lawyer," Jason said as he started to get up.

"Wait," he said. "I'll talk to you."

"Are you willing to talk to us freely without a lawyer?"

"Yes."

"You're waiving your right to have a lawyer present before any questioning? Is that right?" Jeff asked.

"Yes. I don't want a lawyer. I'll answer your questions," he insisted.

Jason looked over at Jeff and smiled. Now, maybe they could get somewhere, he thought.

"Where's Jackson?"

"I don't know."

"How long have you been hiding him?"

"About two or three days."

"Where's his partner?"

"I don't know anything about no partner."

"Did you know that he robbed a blind lady?"

"No. I didn't know nothin' about it until you said something about it in the bar."

"Then what do you know?" Jason asked, his frustration with McDonnally showing in his voice.

"About three days ago, Jackson came to me and asked me to put him up in the back room. He said he needed a place to hide for a little while."

"Did he say why he needed a place to hide?"

"He said that some guy he owed money to was looking for him. That's why I asked you if he owed you money when you came in looking for him. I thought you was the guy."

"How long have you known Jackson?"

"About a year or two, I guess."

"You know any of his friends?"

"No. He hasn't ever come to the bar with anyone. He always comes in alone."

"You ever see him talking with anyone in the bar?"

McDonnally thought for a minute. Suddenly his eyes lit up as if he remembered something that might get Jason to back off a little.

"I saw him talking to the lady that left the credit card."

"You saw him talking to the lady who said she was Kandace Clarke?"

"Yeah. They seemed pretty friendly," he said, pleased that he had come up with something that seemed to interest Lieutenant Barrett.

Jason looked over at Jeff, then back at McDonnally. He wasn't sure if McDonnally was making this up to save his own skin, or if he actually did see Jackson talking to the woman.

"What did this woman look like? Describe her for me."

"Well, she was probably in her late forties. She was short, maybe five-three or five-four. She must have weighed about a hundred and forty to a hundred and fifty pounds, I would guess. She had short curly brown hair with a little gray in it, dark colored eyes and a nose that was a little reddish with dark streaks. From the looks of her, I would say she was a boozer. She drank pretty heavy at the bar, but she could hold her booze. She had a small dark spot, about the size of a quarter, just under her left eye. If you didn't know better, you'd think it was dirt."

Jason suddenly remembered the old bag lady from the alley. He had noticed a dark spot under her left eye. He thought it was dirt, but maybe it was a birthmark. She was shorter than five-four, and looked to be much heavier. She also appeared to be much older than her late forties. The bag lady was closer to sixty, maybe very early seventies, or was she, he thought.

It would not be hard for someone to make themselves look older. The fact that the bag lady appeared shorter could have been due to the fact that she always stood kind of hunched over. Looking heavier could be the result of more layers of clothes. Was it possible that the bag lady was the same woman that was in the bar talking to Jackson, he wondered.

"How was she dressed when she came into the bar?"

McDonnally tipped his head back and looked up at the ceiling. He tried to remember what she was wearing. He looked back at Jason.

"She was wearing dark colored slacks and a flowered blouse under a black winter coat. Oh, and no hat."

Jason tried to remember more details about the bag lady, but nothing seemed to match except the "dirt spot" under her left eye. Was it possible that someone else had such a birthmark? That was not very likely. The thought occurred to Jason that with the difference in their ages, could it be possible he was dealing with two women? The age difference could mean that they were mother and daughter, or some other close relationship like aunt and niece. That was certainly a possibility, but the better and more logical answer seemed to be that both women were the same person.

The more Jason thought about what McDonnally had said, the more he wanted to find out about the bag lady. There was enough information to pull her in for questioning, but that might not be the best move right now. If she thought that the police were on to her, she might run. He decided that it might be best to put the old lady under surveillance in the hope of finding out if she was involved in the attack on Kandace in some way.

Jason took a look at his watch, then looked over at Jeff. He was thinking about what would be the best course of action to take at this moment.

"I'm going to let you return to your bar. You're not to say anything to anybody about what you told us. If you do, Jackson will most likely try to kill you," Jason said in the hope that it would instill enough fear in McDonnally to keep him quiet.

"I won't say nothin'," he assured Jason.

"I wouldn't try to disappear, either," Jason warned him. "If you do, I will have you hunted down. I'll come down on you so hard that you won't see the light of day for years."

"I understand," he replied nervously.

"I'm going to have someone watching every move you make. You step out of line just one inch and you'll be in jail so fast you won't know what happened to you. You understand?"

"Yes, I understand."

"Get out of here," Jason demanded, then watched as he stood up.

McDonnally looked at Jeff, then back at Jason as if he didn't believe that they were letting him go. Cautiously, he moved toward the door, looking at Jeff. He was almost sure that Jeff would stop him before he could get out the door.

As McDonnally stepped up to the door, Jeff stepped aside to let him pass. He glanced over at Jason to see if he should stop McDonnally, or let him go. He saw Jason motion for him to let McDonnally leave.

Once McDonnally was gone, Jeff turned back toward Jason.

"Do you think that was a smart move, Jason?"

"I'm not sure, but I'm going with my gut feeling on this one."

"You want to fill me in on what your gut feeling has to say?"

"My gut tells me that the old bag lady that found Miss Clarke's briefcase and purse had something to do with the attack on her. I don't know what she had to do with it, but there's a connection there some place."

"What about McDonnally?"

"I want him watched. Keep surveillance on him twenty-four hours a day. If Jackson comes around, arrest him."

"Do you think that's a good idea?"

"What's on your mind?"

"If we arrest Jackson on sight, won't that give away the fact that we're watching McDonnally's bar? If anyone else is involved, it might scare them off."

"I see your point. Okay. Keep a watch on the bar and see what you can find out about everyone who goes in or out. If Jackson shows up, try to follow him and have him picked up away from the bar."

"Will do," Jeff replied. "Where are you going?"

"I'm going back to my apartment and check on Miss Clarke. Give me a call if anything comes up."

"Okay," Jeff replied then left Jason in the interrogation room with his thoughts.

Jason sat back down at the table. He let his thoughts go back to the night he first saw the old bag lady. He tried to review in his mind what he saw in an effort to recall some little detail that he might have overlooked. Although the descriptions of the two women were different, the idea that they were one and the same person kept coming to mind. There had to be a reason that he couldn't get that idea out of his mind.

After thinking about it for several minutes and coming up with no clear answer, he decided to go home. After all, Kandace was waiting for him. That thought seemed to please him. It had been years since he had anyone waiting for him to come home.

Jason left the police department and drove toward his apartment. He found himself turning down a street that would take him past the place where Kandace had been attacked. As he came to the alley, he slowed down and stopped. He took a minute or so to look down the alley.

While he looked, a thought came to mind. He reached down and picked up the mike to his two-way radio.

"Four Adam twenty-seven. Dispatch," Jason said into the mike.

"Four Adam twenty-seven."

"Patch me to records, please."

"Roger."

He had to wait only a few moments before his call was patched through.

"This is records. May I help you?"

"This is Lieutenant Barrett. I need to know how many muggings have occurred in the area where

Miss Kandace Clarke was attacked, say in the past six months. Include about a ten block area."

"How soon do you need that information?"

"Yesterday," Jason replied.

"It will take me about an hour, maybe longer, to get it together."

"That'll be fine. As soon as you have that information, call me at my home."

"Will do."

"Thanks," Jason said then ended the conversation.

Jason took another look down the alley. The alley appeared empty. He checked traffic, then pulled out and started on down the street again.

* * * *

Within a few minutes, he pulled into the parking lot of his apartment. He looked up at the balcony to his apartment and saw lights on in the kitchen. He wondered what Kandace was doing. He wondered if she had fixed dinner, or if she was simply waiting for him to come home.

He got out of his car and started up the stairs to his apartment. He could hear music coming from his apartment as he reached out to unlock the door. As he opened the door and stepped inside, he could see Kandace in the kitchen. He also noticed the table was set.

"Hello," he called out in the hope that he wouldn't frighten her.

"Oh, hi. I didn't hear you come in. I guess I have the music up a little loud," she apologized.

"No, that's okay. It's been a long time since I've heard that music."

"You like it?" she asked as she reached out and put her hand on the door jam from the kitchen.

"Sure. I just haven't heard it for a long time."

"That was really a dumb question. Of course you would like it. It's your tape," she said feeling foolish.

"What are we having for dinner? Whatever it is, it sure smells good," he said as he hung up his coat.

"I'm not one hundred percent sure. If the meat on the plate is what I thought it was, we are having Swiss steak made with mushroom sauce. Corn and mashed potatoes, unless I just peeled tomatoes by mistake," she laughed.

Jason could not help but smile. At least she had a sense of humor. It fascinated him that she could do these things without being able to see. The one thing that concerned him was how she kept from burning herself on the hot stove.

"The meat on the plate was round steak, just right for Swiss steak. From the smell, it should be very good. I didn't have any tomatoes left, so you probably peeled potatoes."

"Good. It will be ready as soon as you wash up."

"I'll be right back."

Jason went into the bathroom and washed up. When he returned to the kitchen, he saw her bending over the oven. His first thought was to help her, but he watched her instead. He watched her move her hand slowly toward the dish. She was wearing his kitchen mittens. Being very careful, she picked up the dish and pulled it out of the oven.

"I put a hot pad on the table. Would you mind taking this and putting it on the table. There's a couple of pan holders next to the sink."

"Of course not," he replied as he looked over and saw the pan holders right where she said they would be.

He picked up the holders, then took the dish from her. As he set the dish on the hot pad on the table, he noticed that the table was nicely set. Looking at how neat it was, he realized that it must have taken her half the afternoon just to set the table.

"The table sure looks nice."

"Thank you. I would have put a tablecloth on and some candles, but I didn't know where to find them," she said.

"I don't know if I have any candles, I guess we'll have to get some. I do have a tablecloth if I can remember where I put it."

Kandace laughed at his effort to make her feel more at ease.

"By the way, what's the occasion?" Jason asked.

"Nothing really. I just thought that since you were kind enough to put up with me these past few days, the least I could do is to be useful."

"You didn't have to do this, but I'm glad you did. It's been a long time since I've had Swiss steak."

"I'm glad."

"What can I do to help you?"

"You can mash the potatoes, if you like."

"Okay."

Jason took the pan of potatoes off the stove. While he mashed the potatoes, he watched as Kandace finished preparing the rest of the meal. He found that she was quite capable in the kitchen. She poured his milk without spilling it, put the corn in a serving dish without spilling it, and did a very good job of getting empty pots and pans into the sink where they would not be in the way.

When all was done, they sat down at the table to eat dinner. After dinner, Jason helped her clean up the kitchen and put things away. When they were finished, he slipped his arm around her narrow waist.

"One thing has puzzled me all evening," he said as he guided her into the living room.

"What's that?" she asked as she enjoyed the feel of his arm around her.

"How did you find the mushroom soup to make the sauce for the steak?"

"You told me where it was."

"I told you?" he said with surprise as he guided her to the sofa.

"Yes," she replied as she sat down. "You told me the other night when I tried to put a glass on that shelve."

"You remembered that?"

"I have to remember things like that. I can't see where I'm putting things, so I have to remember where they are."

"Of course," he replied a little embarrassed that he had not thought of that.

Kandace could sense his embarrassment. She had not intended to embarrass him, only to explain.

"Shall we watch Jeopardy," she said with a smile and patted the sofa next to her.

"Sure."

Jason sat down next to her and took up the remote. He turned on the television and leaned back. As Jeopardy came on, he glanced over at her. His eyes drifted down to her hand. It was resting in her lap.

He reached over and took her hand in his. She turned and smiled at him, then turned back toward the television. Neither of them said anything.

Kandace found it difficult to concentrate on the program. The feel of Jason's hand in hers was too distracting. She had never had the feelings she was experiencing at that moment from anyone else who had held her hand. She liked it, but she still wasn't sure if it was a good idea. She was still afraid to get too close to him, or let him get too close to her.

Jason felt the warmth of her small hand in his. She was beautiful, kind, and giving. He wondered if she would ever let him get close to her. He wondered what she would do if he put his arm around her and pulled her up against his shoulder. There was only one way to find out.

Jason let go of her hand. He slipped his arm around behind her, resting his hand on her shoulder. Suddenly, without any warning, she snuggled up against him, resting her head on his shoulder. Jason was surprised by her action, but he didn't mind. Maybe, she would let him into her world after all, he thought.

CHAPTER FOURTEEN

Jason had spent the next hour or so watching Jeopardy and one other game show with Kandace's head resting against his shoulder. He had not realized until that very minute that she had dozed off. The fact that she seemed comfortable with him gave him hope that she would be willing to let him into her world.

Jason reached over and turned the volume on the television down so as not to disturb her. He tipped his head back and relaxed, letting his mind wander off into space.

He wondered if Kandace was as comfortable with him as he was with her. Maybe, she was just feeling safe with him, a feeling he was sure that she could not experience in her own apartment after what had happened.

Jason also wondered what would happen to them once she found a place of her own where she could again feel safe. Would she still be willing to spend time with him? Would she want him to call on her?

Suddenly, his thoughts were disturbed by the ringing of his phone. Kandace sat up and looked toward the end of the sofa where the phone sat.

"Sorry," Jason said as he reached for the phone. "Hello."

"Lieutenant Barrett?" the woman's voice on the other end of the line asked.

"Yes."

"I have the information that you requested. It seems that there have been nine muggings in the past four months in the area you requested information on. Six were committed within a four-block area, two more in a six-block area, and one more in an eight-block area. There were two more muggings just outside the ten block area you asked me to cover."

"Thanks," Jason said as he let the information sink into his head.

"A couple of other interesting things came up in my research."

"Oh? What was that?" he asked as he sat up.

"Of the six muggings committed in the four block area, three resulted in the death of the victims. Also, two others were hospitalized, one is still in a coma. But the most interesting find was that five of those attacks were on people who were disabled in some way."

"What?"

"Five of those were. . . . "

"I heard you. I just find it hard to believe. Five of the attacks were on people who were disabled?"

"Yes sir. There was Miss Clarke, who is blind, plus four others. Three men and one woman who were all wheelchair dependent."

"Interesting. It looks like we have a real gem out there."

"Yes, sir."

"Those who were attacked that were disabled, where were they attacked?" he asked as a pattern started to form in his head.

"All five were attacked within two or three blocks of each other."

"You're kidding?

"No, sir."

"That doesn't make any sense. Why would someone bring that kind of attention to themselves? Even a complete idiot would have to know that the news media would eventually pick up on it. That kind of action would enrage the general populous."

"You would think so."

"Unless that's what they want?"

"Sir?"

"Maybe whoever is doing this wants something, or is actually using this as revenge for something that happened to them, or they think happened to them," he said as he thought out loud while trying to make some sense out of all that he had heard.

"That's a possibility, I guess. Is there anything else?"

"No, not right now. Thanks for digging it up for me."

"You're welcome," the woman said, then the phone went dead.

Jason was deep in thought as he slowly hung up the receiver. What would make a person go out and intentionally attack people who are disabled?

"What's going on?" Kandace asked, disturbing his thoughts.

"I don't know, but it seems that we have someone who has it in for people who are disabled. It makes me think that you might not have been just a random target. Whoever is doing this set out to specifically attack you."

"Why would someone do such a thing?"

"That I don't know," Jason admitted.

Kandace snuggled up against Jason as his thoughts turned to the information he had been given. Most often, the criminal doesn't want to draw any more attention to himself than necessary. Whoever was doing it must want the attention, but why?

The case was getting strange. He needed to understand what would motivate someone to attack those considered to be less able to defend themselves. Was it due to their own weakness, and they were taking their frustrations out on those who were considered to be weaker; or was it something else? Was it as simple as the strong shall survive and take from the weak?

Jason didn't think his last thought was the answer. It was not that simple. He knew too many disabled people who were far from weak and far from defenseless.

Jason's thoughts turned to Kandace. Why would someone attack her? Most people would be afraid to attack someone with a large dog, especially a German Shepard. There was no doubt that Chester was a large German Shepard. He must weigh close to ninety pounds and was obviously a very strong dog, Jason thought.

From what Kandace had told him about the incident, Chester let the attackers know that he was going to protect Kandace by growling and standing between them. There was also the fact that Chester put up a good fight when the attackers didn't back off. There was always the possibility that the attackers didn't think she would let the dog loose, but that didn't seem likely, either.

Kandace was leaning against his side, but she was not asleep now. She could sense that Jason was deep in thought. She wanted to know what he was thinking, but did not want to disturb his thoughts, not just yet. She had some thoughts of her own.

Her thoughts had turned to her apartment. She knew that she would not be able to return there without someone with her. She also knew that she would never feel safe there again. There was no doubt in her mind that she would need to move, and that she would need someone to help her. But even if she moved, would she ever feel safe again, she wondered. Would she ever be able to feel safe knowing that there were people out there making targets of the disabled?

That thought caused her to think of Jason. She had never felt as safe as she felt right now. Leaning against his side reassured her that she was safe, at least for now.

Jason could sense that she was still awake. He turned and looked at her.

"Are you okay?" he asked.

"Yes. I was just thinking about what you said. Do you think that these people are intentionally attacking people with disabilities, or that it was just a coincidence?"

"I'm not sure, but it's beginning to look like it is intentional."

"What kind of a person would do such a thing?"

"What kind of person robs anyone?"

"I see your point," Kandace said with a sigh.

"What do you say that we forget about this for tonight," Jason suggested.

"What would you like to do?"

"Well, I was thinking that I might like to kiss you. But if that is not a possibility, than maybe you would tell me what you plan to do when this is over.

"The kiss doesn't sound too bad. I might not mind that, but we could still talk," she replied with a grin.

"Great," he replied as he reached out and put his hand on her cheek.

As he gently guided her closer, he leaned down until his lips met hers. It was a warm gentle kiss meant to let her know that he cared very much for her, but he was willing to take it slow if that is what she wanted.

It turned out to be a long kiss that Kandace found very much to her liking. The feel of his hand on her cheek, and his lips against hers, sent a feeling of desire through her. For the first time, she felt that it was right. She had not enjoyed that feeling for a very long time. Her heart was telling her that she was doing the right thing, but her head was still trying to tell her to use caution.

Jason thought he felt a slight hesitation on her part. It caused him to wonder if he was pressing her a little too much. He decided that he should change his approach and broke off the kiss.

Kandace was a little surprised that he broke off the kiss, but it did give her a chance to take a breath. She found herself breathing rather rapidly. She could not remember a time when such a tender kiss had affected her so much.

Jason was affected by the kiss, too. It took him a minute to catch his breath. As he looked at her face, he wondered if she did the same things on a date as other woman. The more he thought about it, the more he was sure that she would want to be treated like any other woman.

"I have an idea," he blurted out, not taking time to think about it.

"What is your idea," she said with a bit of a laugh.

"It's about three or four blocks to a place that has the best ice cream sundaes in town. I know it's a little cold out tonight, but how would you like to walk over there for some ice cream?"

"If it's cold outside, I might prefer a cup of hot coffee or hot chocolate."

"Okay. That sounds good, too. I take it you wouldn't mind going for a walk with me, then?"

"Not at all. I would like that very much," she replied with a smile.

"Then that settles it. I'll get our coats."

"I'll be with you in a minute," she said as she stood up, found her way around the coffee table and walked into the bedroom.

Jason got their coats and gloves, then put them on the back of a chair. As he waited, he looked toward the bedroom door and thought about her. She must feel safe with me, he thought. Otherwise, she wouldn't be so willing to go outside.

"I feel terrible," she said as she came out of the bedroom.

"What's the matter?" It was clear by the sound of Jason's voice that he was concerned about her.

"I haven't given Chester hardly a thought today."

"I'm sure he's doing fine. Besides, I'm sure that he is sleeping a lot, he was hurt pretty bad."

"Can we go by and see him tomorrow?" she asked.

"Of course. We'll go first thing in the morning."

"Thank you," Kandace replied.

"You ready to go?"

"Yes."

She walked toward the sound of his voice. When she got close to him, he let her know where he was standing.

"If you'll turn around, I'll help you with your coat."

"I can do it," she replied.

"I know you can, but a gentleman always helps a lady with her coat."

"Yes, of course," she replied as she turned around.

Jason helped her with her coat, then handed her gloves to her. He then put on his own coat and gloves. After guiding her hand to his arm, he guided her out of the apartment and down the stairs.

Once outside he walked along with her holding onto his arm. He told her when to step down for a curb, when to step up and when to stop, but most of the time they just walked along the sidewalk arm in arm like any other couple.

"It is a little nippy out tonight," Kandace said as she reached over and took hold of his arm with her other hand.

"Is it too cold? We can go back if you want."

"No. We're almost there."

Jason looked at her. He wondered how she knew that. Then he remembered that he had told her that it was three or four blocks from his apartment, and she would be making mental notes of how many streets they had crossed.

When they arrived at the Ice Cream Parlor, Jason held the door for her. Once inside, he guided her to a table where they sat down. A college girl came over to their table.

"Would you like a menu?"

"I don't think so. What would you like?" Jason asked Kandace.

"I think I would like a cup of hot black coffee. I'm a little too cold to have ice cream," Kandace replied.

"Two black coffees, please," Jason said, then watched the waitress leave.

"What's it like here? It smells delicious."

Jason looked around the place, then began to describe it to her. He left little out. He even described the few people who were in the store. When he was finished describing the place, he looked at her sitting across the table from him.

"And there's this beautiful woman sitting across the table from me. Her eyes are sparkling, her cheeks are rosy and her nose looks a little red."

Kandace grinned as she put her hand over her nose. She liked the way he talked and the pleasant, almost soothing tone of his voice. Although she was a little embarrassed about the red nose, it did show her that he cared about her very much.

"Now her face is a little red. I'm sorry. I didn't mean to embarrass you."

"That's all right," she said. "I - - -."

She was about to say more, but she was interrupted by the waitress bringing their coffee. As soon as the waitress set the coffee on the table, she left.

"Your coffee is directly in front of you," Jason said without giving it a thought.

But Kandace thought about it. It was a reminder of how much of a burden she could be. The last thing she wanted to be was a burden to anyone. He would always have to tell her where everything was on the table, or she might accidentally knock something over. Would he be willing to do that for her every time they went out, every time they had dinner together when she didn't set the table? Would he remember to put things back where he got them so that she could find them? Would he remember not to move the furniture? A dangerous thing to do with a blind person walking around.

Jason watched her as she wrapped her hands around the warm coffee cup. As she lifted the coffee to her soft lips, he was sure that he detected a change in her. It was hard to see, but he was sure it was there. It caused him to wonder what was going on in her mind.

"What are you thinking about?" he asked softly.

Kandace looked across the table at him. Although she could not see him, she could sense that he had a worried look on his face. She wanted to tell him what was on her mind, but it didn't seem like the right time or place.

"Are you worried about Chester?" Jason suggested when she didn't answer him.

"Yes," she replied, glad that he had given her an easy out.

"He will be fine."

"I know. It's...it's just that I need him so much."

"Excuse me, but Kandace it's me, Marsha."

Jason looked up at the woman who interrupted them. She was standing just a few feet from the table. She looked from Kandace to Jason, then back to Kandace.

"Oh, hi, Marsha."

"We've been worried about you. We heard about - - - you know."

"I'm fine. I'll be back to work tomorrow."

"Good. Do you need someone to come get you?"

"That won't be necessary," Jason said. "I'll see to it that she gets to work."

"Oh, I'm sorry. Marsha, this is Lieutenant Barrett of the police department."

"Hi," she said with a big smile.

"Nice to meet you, Marsha."

"Well, I'll see you tomorrow, then."

"Okay," Kandace said.

Kandace could hear the sound of Marsha's shoes on the hard floor as she left the store. She turned toward Jason. She wanted to tell him that he did not need to look after her, but she knew that was just what she did need.

"I hope you don't mind that I told her I would take you to work. I thought you might prefer that she doesn't know you're staying at my apartment. It might be embarrassing for you to explain."

"Thank you. But it would give them something to talk about if they did know," she said with a grin.

"I'm sure it would do that, but I didn't think you would want that."

"No, I really wouldn't. I'm sorry that you have gotten stuck with the job of looking after me."

"I'm not," Jason said as he reached across the table and put his hand over hers.

Kandace could feel the warmth of his hand as he touched her hand. Just his touch made her breath catch and her heart race. What was it about him that made him so much different from other men she had dated, she asked herself.

While still holding hands, they slowly drank the warm liquid from their cups. Jason continued to watch her. She seemed nervous to him. He wondered what it was that made her nervous.

When Jason saw that she had finished her coffee, he thought that they should head back to his apartment. He was reluctant to go, but he was sure that it was gradually getting colder outside. If he waited too much longer, the walk home could be a very cold one. He thought about calling for a cab, but decided to leave that up to Kandace.

"Are you ready to go?"

"Whenever you are."

"Would you like me to call a cab? It's pretty cold out."

"I don't think that will be necessary. It won't be too bad if we move right along. Besides, I like winter."

"Okay, but if you get cold, we can stop at a convenience store to warm up, or call a cab."

"Okay."

Kandace took him by the arm and let him lead her outside. The cold evening air felt good on her face. It was a little colder than when they had come, but still not so bad that a short walk would be that uncomfortable.

Jason moved her right along. They walked a little faster going back to Jason's apartment. Kandace did not seem to mind. It helped her stay warm.

Once they returned to his apartment, he helped her with her coat. He hung their coats in the closet, then joined her on the sofa.

"Would you like something to warm you up, like a cup of coffee or some hot chocolate?" he asked.

"Hot chocolate sounds good."

"I'll fix it," he said as he stood up.

Kandace followed him as far as the kitchen door. She stood in the doorway. Jason was sure that she wanted to say something, but wasn't sure how to get her started. He decided to start out on a lighter note.

"Well, I know I'm not as well trained as Chester, but how did I do for my first time out?"

"You did just fine. Chester would be proud of you. I'm sure that he would be pleased at the patience you have with me."

"That makes me feel a lot better, but tomorrow when we see him, you can tell him that I'm not trying to take his job away from him."

Kandace was not sure how to take what he had said. Did he mean that he would be glad when he was rid of her? Was he already getting tired of looking out for her?

Jason glanced over at Kandace. He thought he noticed sadness in her face. He wondered what it was that was bothering her. After a moment's thought, he was sure it was her thoughts of Chester that made her feel sad.

"Chester will be all right. You'll have him back before you know it," he said in an effort to get her to feel better.

"I know," she replied in a whisper.

"Then what's the matter?"

Jason did not wait for a reply. He walked over to her and took her in his arms. As he wrapped his arms around her, she laid her head on his shoulder. He could tell that she was crying. He wasn't sure what to do, so he just stood there and held her. After a few minutes, he leaned back, took her chin in his fingers and lifted her head up. He looked into her eyes.

"Tell me what's wrong," he said in a whisper.

She let out a sigh. She had no business expecting him to understand how she felt. After all, he was just looking after her until they found her attackers. She had no right to expect anything more.

"Come on, there isn't anything that you can't tell me."

She didn't want to tell him that she loved him and end up making a fool of herself because he didn't love her in return. She wouldn't allow herself to put that kind of pressure on him. He had to love her because he wanted to, not because she wanted him to. She would just be a burden to him, and she couldn't do that to him. It was best to just stop now before it went too far.

Kandace took a deep breath, put her hands on his shoulders and lightly pushed him away. It was not what she wanted to do, but she was sure that it was for the best.

"I'm kind of tired. I think I should go to bed. You don't have to see that I get to work tomorrow. I can call a cab," she said in a firm but soft voice.

"I'd be glad to take you to work."

"That won't be necessary," she said as she turned and walked back into the living room.

Jason followed her as far as the kitchen door. From there, he watched her go into the bedroom and close the door. He was confused. He didn't understand her actions.

Jason turned around and walked over to the stove. He shut it off, then went into the living room. Her sudden change in attitude had caught him off guard. He could not figure out what was the cause.

After giving it some thought, he wondered if the pressures of all that had happened was just getting to her. When she thought of Chester, maybe it was just too much.

That sort of made sense to Jason, but he still needed more answers. He thought about going to the bedroom door and knocking on it. If she answered, what would he say? He decided that it would be better if he just went to sleep. Maybe she would feel more like talking in the morning.

Jason got ready for bed and curled up on the sofa. Time passed slowly. He rolled over on his back and looked up at the ceiling. His thoughts were of the woman in the next room.

Kandace quickly got ready for bed and laid down, pulling the covers over her. She wanted so much to have him hold her, but the idea that she might be a burden to him was overpowering her wishes. She buried her face in the pillow and cried.

CHAPTER FIFTEEN

The hours of the night passed slowly for Kandace. She had cried for a long time. She could not find the sleep that she had hoped would cause her mind to stop thinking about Jason and how good it felt to be held in his arms. In the very next room was the man she wanted more than anything she could remember, but she was letting him slip away. She was forcing him out of her life in an effort to avoid the risk to love and to be loved.

Suddenly, she remembered what her father had told her just shortly after she became blind. Her father had been the one person in her life who really believed in her and seemed to understand her. He believed that she could still have a full and happy life, even without sight.

"Just because you can't see doesn't mean you can't have everything you want out of life," her father had told her. "It's just that sometimes you might have to work at it a little harder to get it."

Kandace knew what she wanted. She wanted to find out if Jason was the one man in her life that would mean everything to her. And if he was the one man who would love her in spite of her blindness. She wanted to be held, to be kissed, and to be loved by him. She had already come to accept the fact that she loved him. In fact, she loved him so much that she didn't want to be a burden to him.

Meanwhile, Jason laid on the sofa. His mind was playing havoc with him. He would try to think about Jackson and the old bag lady in an effort to solve the case, but would inevitably end up thinking about Kandace and how he felt about her. It would have been the natural thing to do since she had been the victim, but that was not how he thought of her. He thought of her as the one woman who could make his life complete. The one woman he could love for the rest of his life.

Each time he tried to think of the case, his mind turned on him and he would end up thinking about how it felt to hold her in his arms. He would remember how it felt to have her body pressed against him and how it felt to press his lips against hers.

There was no doubt that she was all woman. Yet, he had no illusions about her. The fact that she was blind would mean that he would have to make some adjustments in his lifestyle if there was any possibility of a lasting relationship. But even if she wasn't blind, people have to make adjustments, he thought.

Once again he tried to turn his thoughts back to those who attacked her, but it was difficult. He wondered if he might unconsciously be dragging his feet a little because he didn't want her to move into another apartment and not need him any more. He would not want that to be the case, he could not allow that to happen. There was no mistake about it. He knew what he had to do.

Starting first thing tomorrow morning, he would dive into the case at full speed. He set his mind to putting tomorrow in order, setting his priorities.

First of all, he would take her to see Chester. When she was finished there, he would take her to work. While she was at work, he would check out every possible lead he had and even check out his hunches. He would find Jackson and the old bag lady and get to the bottom of it.

Jason's thoughts were suddenly interrupted by the soft sound of footsteps in the silence of the night. He heard the door to his bedroom open. Turning his head, he could see Kandace standing in the bedroom door. There was a little light coming in the window from outside and it silhouetted her in the doorway.

"Jason?" she called out in a faint whisper."

"Yes?"

"I'm not disturbing you, am I?"

"No, of course not. What is it?"

"Would you mind if I come and sit with you for a little while?"

Jason sat up on the sofa and watched her as she walked toward him. When she got to the sofa,

Jason reached up and took her hand. He guided her to the sofa beside him.

Kandace sat down beside him. He did not let go of her hand, and she was glad of that. She wanted him to touch her, even if it was just to hold her hand.

"What's the matter?" Jason asked.

"I'm sorry about this evening," she said softly.

"It's okay."

"No, it's not. I haven't been entirely fair to you."

"I don't understand."

"It's hard to explain," she said, then took a deep sigh.

Jason just sat there and gently squeezed her hand. He wanted to know what was on her mind, but he didn't want to push her. Whatever she had to say had to come when she was ready.

"I get the feeling that you care about me," she started out. "If I am wrong, please tell me now."

"No, you are not wrong. I do care about you very much," he replied.

"I care about you, but..." she hesitated for a moment.

"But what? Are you afraid that the fact you're blind will cause me to like you less?"

"No. I'm afraid that my blindness will become a burden to you. Maybe not today, maybe not tomorrow, but some day."

"Are you sure that's what you are afraid of?"

"Yes," she replied wondering what he might be getting at.

"Whatever happens between us, there will be adjustments to be made by both of us. No matter what our relationship becomes, there will be times when we will be a burden to each other. Not just because you're blind, but because that is the way it is with everybody."

"But my blindness will make it harder."

"Possibly. But I think your blindness will simply mean that I have to make a few adjustments in the way I do things, but those are little things. I'm talking about the adjustments that any couple has to make in getting to know each other's needs and wants."

Kandace thought about what he was saying. She understood him, but she was having a hard time believing what he was saying. If she wanted him, she knew what she was going to have to do. She was going to have to give him a chance. She was going to have to take the risk of letting him into her life. She could not let the one man that had given her a chance to love, and to be loved, simply slip away from her. She would have to take the risk.

"Jason?"

"Yes?"

"Will you kiss me?"

Jason did not answer. Instead, he reached over and put his hand on her cheek. Slowly, and carefully, he drew her toward him until their lips met.

Kandace allowed herself to relax and enjoy the feel of his lips against hers. The kiss lasted for only a moment or two, but it was enough to let Kandace know that Jason cared very much for her.

As she drew back, a soft smile came over her face. Jason looked at her. Even in the darkness of the living room, he could see the sparkle in her eyes. It struck him as strange that she could have such beautiful eyes, yet she could not see him.

Kandace raised her hands up and lightly touched Jason's face. He closed his eyes and let her fingers lightly drift over the curves of his face; the bridge of his nose, the outline of his brow, the line of his hair and the tiny wrinkles around his eyes and mouth.

"You are very handsome," she whispered softly.

"And you are very beautiful," he replied.

Kandace slid her fingers off his face and rested her hands on his bare shoulders. Jason reached out and drew her to him. As she tipped her head back slightly, he leaned down and their lips met again, only it was a much more passionate kiss.

Jason could feel the warmth of her body through her nightgown, and the firmness of her breasts against his chest. She moaned softly as he slid his hands up her back to her shoulders. He drew back and looked at her face.

"Is something wrong?" she asked, not sure why he drew back from her.

"No, there is nothing wrong. Everything is very right," he replied. "It's just that I'm sitting on my sofa in the middle of the night in my undershorts, holding in my arms the most beautiful woman I think I have ever met. And the beautiful woman is in a shear, very sexy nightgown. Now, what do you think is wrong with this picture?"

"Let me guess. Could it be the sofa?"

"It could be, but I'm not sure how the beautiful woman would want to change the picture."

"She might like it if you would take her to your bed and spend the night with her."

"Are you sure that's what you want?" he asked in a whisper.

"Yes," she replied in a hushed, almost inaudible voice.

Jason took his arms from around her and stood up. He reached down and took hold of her hand.

Kandace stood up and let him lead her into the bedroom. Once inside the room, she let go of his hand. In the dimly lit room, she reached up and slowly slipped the shoulder straps of her nightgown off her shoulders, one at a time. She then let her nightgown cascade down her shapely body and fall to the floor at her feet.

Jason stood silently watching her as the nightgown fell. She was so beautiful standing in front of him completely naked. He quickly removed his undershorts, then reached out and took her hand.

He thought about taking her in his arms, but led her to the side of the bed instead. When she touched the side of the bed, he let go of her hand and watched her as she climbed into his bed.

Kandace laid down on her back and held the covers up for him. He climbed in beside her. As he rolled over to her, she pulled the covers over him. She let him take her in his arms and rolled up against him.

Jason liked the feel of her warm body against him. She rested her head on his shoulder, while he tucked her up against him.

Kandace curled one of her shapely legs over his and rested her arm across his chest. She gently ran her fingers through the hair on his chest. She tipped her head up as if she was looking at him.

"You feel good," she whispered.

"So do you," he replied as he lightly stroked her smooth back.

"I love you," she whispered so softly he almost did not hear her.

Jason slid his hand up her side and over one of her firm breasts. She moaned softly as he gently cupped her breast.

"Love me," she whispered.

It was a time for them to have alone, a time to touch, to feel, to love. Together, they drifted off in that safe, secure world where only the two of them could go. It was a place where they could be that no one else could be.

* * * *

Jason woke as a few rays of sunshine slipped past the edge of the bedroom curtain. As the sleep cleared from his head, he realized he was not alone in his bed. It was then that he remembered what had taken place last night.

He turned and looked at Kandace. She looked so much at peace as she lay sleeping on the other side of his bed that he didn't want to disturb her.

He took a minute to look at her. She was lying on her side facing toward him, her head resting on the pillow, her hands tucked under the pillow. Her bare shoulders showed her smooth soft skin, and the sheet that covered her clung to her shapely figure.

As his eyes returned to her face, he noticed what seemed to be a slight smile on her lips. He had to smile to himself as he watched her sleep.

A glance at the clock told him that it would be time to get up soon. He reached up and shut off the alarm so that it would not disturb her. He then eased himself out of bed so as not to wake her, and went into the bathroom.

When he returned from the bathroom, he found Kandace lying on her back. She had her eyes open and seemed to be looking up at the ceiling.

"Good morning," Jason said as he looked at her.

"Good morning," she replied with a smile. "What time is it?"

"Time to get up. It's almost seven-thirty."

"Oh."

"Did you sleep well?"

"Oh, yes," she replied in a whisper.

"If you don't mind, I would like to have a morning kiss, then I will get out of your way so you can get dressed."

"I don't mind at all."

Jason leaned over the bed. He lowered himself until his lips touched hers. He gave her a light kiss, then stood up.

"Is that all I get?" she asked softly.

"You might get more than that if I continue to kiss you when you look like you do."

"What do I look like?"

Jason took a second to look her over before he answered.

"You look sexy as hell."

"Do I really?" she asked with a smile.

"I think I better go fix breakfast before I decide to climb back in bed with you."

"I love you," she whispered as she heard him leave the room.

Kandace liked the sound of his voice when he was being playful. She remembered how beautiful last night had been with him. She felt as sexy as he seemed to think she looked. She was almost floating on air as she thought of him.

But her thoughts were suddenly interrupted by the sound of the telephone ringing in the other room. The phone seemed to be a reminder of why she was in his apartment in the first place.

"Hello."

"Jason, this is Jeff. We think we may have found Jackson's associate in the attack on Miss Clarke."

"Where?"

"We found a man's body in a drainage ditch last night. It was found behind some apartments just off Shields and Drake Road."

"What makes you think it's the man we're looking for?"

"He was wearing a flannel shirt with the sleeve of the right arm torn. When they removed the shirt at the morgue, his arm showed that a rather large dog had bitten him. From what they said, the bite was deep and violent. The dog that bit him actually broke one of the bones in his lower arm."

"How come it took so long for you to call me?"

"I just found out about the dog bite a few minutes ago."

"What was the cause of death?"

"It looks like a very thin screwdriver, or an ice pick, neatly shoved into his back between the third and fourth ribs. A very neat job. We'll know more after the autopsy is done."

"I want you to go out to the scene and go over the area with a fine tooth comb. I want nothing left that we don't know about. I've got a couple of things to do, then I'm going to find that old bag lady. Keep me posted."

"Will do."

As Jason hung up the phone, he looked up and saw Kandace standing in the bedroom door. She was clutching the front of her robe, holding it tightly closed. He could see by the look on her face that she knew the phone call had something to do with her.

"That was Jeff, wasn't it?"

"Yes. They think they found one of the men who attacked you."

"Are they sure?"

"Pretty sure. His right arm showed signs of a severe dog bite. We think Chester might have inflicted the wound."

"Is the man dead?"

"Yes."

Jason watched the expression on her face. He almost expected to see some sigh of relief, but instead he saw her tip her head down and look at the floor. He quickly went to her and wrapped her in his arms.

"Everything's going to be all right," he said in an effort to console her.

Kandace rested her head against Jason's shoulder. How long was it going to continue? How long was she going to be frightened every time the phone rang?

Jason could feel the tension in her body. He wanted to make it all go away, but he couldn't. All he could do was hunt for her attackers and get them put away.

"I love you," he whispered softly in her ear. "I won't let anything happen to you, ever."

Kandace wrapped her arms around his waist and squeezed him against her. When she released him, she tipped her head up.

"I love you, too."

Jason leaned down and kissed her. The kiss was light at first, but soon became a more passionate kiss. When it was over, Jason looked down at her.

"You better get dressed," he suggested.

"Okay," she replied reluctantly.

Jason let go of her and watched her as she went back to the bedroom. As soon as the door closed, he went out to the kitchen to fix breakfast.

By the time breakfast was ready and on the table, Kandace was coming into the kitchen. She sat down at the table. Jason set a plate of bacon and eggs in front of her, then sat down.

"Your juice is at ten o'clock, coffee at two. On the plate, you have toast at three, eggs at six and bacon at about ten."

Listening to Jason tell her where everything was in front of her reminded her that she could be a burden to him. She knew that this was the way it would have to be if he was going to do things for her. But as she thought about last night, and how much pleasure they had given each other, she could not help but think that it was a little thing, one of those little adjustments that Jason said they would have to make.

"What are you thinking," Jason asked as he noticed the worried look on her face change to a more contented look.

"I was thinking about what you said about having to make adjustments."

"What about it?"

"Oh, nothing. I was just thinking about it," she replied with a smile.

"Oh. Well, finish up so we can go see Chester."

"I could take a cab if you have other things you have to attend to."

"No, I'll take you. Besides, I need to get acquainted with him if he's going to be staying here."

Kandace stopped and looked toward him. She wished more than anything that she could see his face in the hope of being able to tell what he really meant. Did he mean that Chester would be staying until she found a new place to stay, or was Jason thinking in terms of a longer stay?

"Jason?"

"Yeah?"

"What did you mean by that?"

She was almost afraid to ask. Her doubts and fears about having a relationship with anyone had drifted back into her mind.

"We can't leave him at the vet's forever. He will be ready to be released soon. He'll need a place to recuperate until he's ready to lead you around again."

"Oh," she said, a little disappointed with his answer.

Kandace finished her breakfast, then helped clear the table. When they were done, Jason helped her with her coat and led her to the car. As they drove to the vet's office, Kandace did not say anything. She simply sat facing forward as if she were looking out the window.

Jason glanced over at her a couple of times, but didn't say anything. He was sure that she was worried about Chester.

CHAPTER SIXTEEN

Chester was awake when Kandace and Jason arrived at the veterinarian's office. He seemed to be doing much better. As Kandace lightly rubbed his head and ears, Jason stood by and watched. It was easy for Jason to see that a dog that large would be able to inflict severe wounds on a person if he had a mind to do so. The way Chester was reacting to Kandace, he was sure the dog would if he thought his mistress was in danger.

It was clear that Chester was feeling much better as he licked Kandace's hand. Even his tail wagged as a way of letting her know that he was going to be fine.

"Would you like to pet him?" Kandace asked.

"Sure," Jason replied as he stepped up closer to Kandace.

Kandace reached out and Jason put his hand in hers. She guided Jason's hand to the dog's head.

"Friend," she instructed the dog.

"Good boy," Jason said as he lightly patted the dog's head.

Jason wasn't sure, but it seemed Chester remembered him from the night of the attack. He wagged his tail and let Jason rub his fur. Chester sniffed Jason's hand, then licked it.

"Well, he either likes me a lot, or he's tasting me to see if I'm worth eating," Jason said with a chuckle.

"Is he licking your hand?"

"Yes."

"He likes you. Do you suppose he remembers you?"

"He might. I spent a few minutes talking to him before they brought him over here. We better have a talk with the vet."

"Okay. You be a good boy. I'll see you later," Kandace said as she rubbed his ears.

Jason guided Kandace's hand to his arm, then led her out into the office. He escorted her to a chair, then went up to the counter.

"Could we talk to the doctor who is taking care of the Seeing Eye Dog?"

"Yes, of course," the young woman said.

Jason walked back to Kandace and sat down beside her. He no more than sat down when a tall man in a white smock came into the lobby.

"I'm Doctor Roth. Please don't get up."

"I'm Lieutenant Barrett of the Fort Collins Police Department, and this is Miss Kandace Clarke, the owner of the Seeing Eye dog, Chester."

"I'm sure you're interested in how Chester is doing. It was a little touch and go the first night, but he is a strong dog. He has a couple of broken ribs and the kicking he received bruised his lungs.

The rest of his injuries are fairly minor, a few cuts and bruises."

"Will he recover totally?" Kandace asked.

She held onto Jason's arm. He could feel the tension in her as she waited for an answer. He was concerned about the dog as well.

"I think he will, but it will take some time. I don't know much about dogs like him, I mean as far as their training is concerned. I don't know if this will affect his ability as a Seeing Eye Dog, or not."

"I don't care as long as he will be okay," Kandace declared.

"I'm sure he will be a healthy dog again. You should be able to take him home in a day or two, but he will not be able to do anything strenuous for probably, oh, a week or so."

"Thanks, Doc," Jason said.

"I'm glad I could help. You're welcome to come see him any time. Letting him know that you love him will help him get better faster," Doctor Roth said with a smile.

"Thank you, Doctor," Kandace replied.

"We'd better get you to work. I have things I have to do today," Jason said as he placed Kandace's hand on his arm.

"I could take a cab, if you have to get going," Kandace suggested as she walked with him out of the doctor's office.

"I'll drop you off at work. It's on my way, anyway."

Kandace didn't argue with him. She liked being with him, but she didn't want to be a bother to him.

Once they got to the car, Jason drove her to her office building. He walked her to her office.

"Are you going to be all right?"

"Sure. Will I see you for lunch?"

Jason had not thought about that. He wondered if there was some place in the building where she could go to eat.

"I don't know if or when I'll be free to have lunch," he said reluctantly, not wanting to disappoint her.

"That's okay. I'll get someone to take me to the lunchroom. I can get something to eat there."

Jason thought he detected a tone of disappointment in her voice. He was not sure if it was because he would not be able to have lunch with her, or if she was feeling like he might be deserting her.

"Here, you'll need some money for lunch in case I can't get back in time," he said as he reached into his wallet.

Jason handed her some money. Kandace was reluctant to take it, but she had not had the opportunity to go to the bank, yet.

"Are you sure you'll be all right?"

"I'll be fine. You go do what you have to do. I'll wait here until you come for me."

"Okay," Jason replied.

He wasn't sure about it, but she knew her way around the office. He was sure that she didn't always have Chester take her everywhere during office time.

"You better go or you will never get done what you have to do, and neither will I," Kandace said as she lovingly pushed him toward the door.

Jason took one last look at her and started out the door. As he turned to go down the hall, he almost ran into the woman that he had seen in the Ice Cream Parlor.

Kandace listened to Jason footsteps as the sound of them faded away. She also heard another set of footsteps come toward her office, a woman's footsteps.

"Good morning, Marsha."

"Good morning. I see your handsome escort brought you to work just as he promised."

"Yes, he did," she said with a smile.

"He's a knockout. I wish I could find a guy like him.

"Looks aren't everything, Marsha," she replied with a smile.

"No, but they sure don't hurt."

"Come on. We have work to do," Kandace said with a grin.

Even though Kandace jumped right into her work in an effort to keep her mind busy, she could not keep from thinking about Jason. Their night together had been wonderful, but she still had a nagging doubt in the back of her mind that things were not going to work out. She wondered if her love for him would be enough to overcome the obstacles.

She had to admit that he had not once objected to taking her anywhere she wanted to go. He had done nothing to indicate that he had anything but love for her, but still her doubts kept creeping into her thoughts. She had taken the risk last night to love and to be loved. Now it was time to give their love a chance to work, a chance to grow.

* * * *

Jason returned to his car. Once inside, he reached for the key to start it, but hesitated. His thoughts were of Kandace. He wondered if she was having second thoughts about last night, he knew that he wasn't. She seemed a little distant. He wondered if last night had been too much too soon for her, and that she was wishing that it had not happened. Tonight, he would have to do something to let her know that he really was in love with her, but for now he owed his time to the police department.

He started the car and pulled away from the curb. He drove to where Kandace had been mugged and turned into the alley. His first order of business was to try to find the old bag lady. He spent the next hour or so driving up and down the alleys and streets of the neighborhood where most of the muggings had occurred. He thought about putting out an APB for her, but that might cause her to go deeper into hiding and make it even harder for him to find her.

During his search for the old bag lady, he saw no one. The streets and alleys were empty. Not a single street person was to be seen. It struck him as strange. Usually, there would be at least one or two of them going through the alleys looking for whatever they could find, but not today.

Jason decided to give up the search for now and see if Jeff had turned up anything. Just as he was about to turn out of the alley onto the street, Jason glanced up at his rear view mirror. He noticed someone behind him. The man looked as if he was hiding behind a Dumpster. Jason was sure that the man was watching him, but why? Why would someone be watching him?

Jason turned out onto the street. As soon as he was out of sight of the man, he stepped on the gas and quickly drove around the block to the other end of the alley. He stopped the car next to the curb just before he got to the alley. Jumping out of the car, he ran to the edge of the building and peeked around the corner. He could see the man standing next to a Dumpster. The man had his back to Jason and was still looking down the alley.

Just as the man turned around, Jason drew his gun from under his coat and stepped out where the man could see him.

"This is the police. I wouldn't try to run if I were you. Put your hands up," Jason ordered him.

The man looked at the gun, then at Jason. He looked as if he was thinking about running, but decided against it. He put his hands up in the air.

"Up against the building and spread 'um."

The man turned and leaned against the building. Jason frisked him, but found no weapons.

"What's your name?"

"Moses."

"Well, Moses, what are you doing here?"

"I was just looking for pop cans."

"You sure you weren't watching me."

"Why would I do that?"

"That's a very good question. Why would you be watching me? Maybe so you could tell somebody that I was here? You think that's a possibility?"

"I guess it could be."

"Then why don't you tell me who wants you to watch me?"

"I ain't watchin' you for nobody."

"I'm not buying that. Who told you to watch me?"

"Nobody," he insisted.

"Okay. I'm going to take you downtown. We'll continue this discussion there."

Jason twisted one of Moses's arms behind his back and put handcuffs on him. Once he had Moses cuffed; he put him in the back seat of the car, then got in behind the wheel.

Jason drove to the police station. While he drove, he would glance up at the mirror to look at Moses's face. Moses looked nervous.

Once they arrived at the police station, Jason took Moses directly to an interrogation room. He sat him down in a chair, then sat down across from him.

"Well, Moses, you ready to talk to me?"

"I can't."

"Why?"

"I'll end up just like Harry."

"Who's Harry?"

"Harry's the guy you guys found last night in the ditch off Shields Street."

"What's Harry's last name?"

"I don't know. I know him as Harry, that's all."

"Tell me what you know about Harry?"

"I can't."

"Do you think Jackson is going to care if you talked or not. He'll kill you if I let you back out on the street. Now talk to me."

Jason could see that Moses was thinking about what he had said. He had no idea if Jackson was a part of it, but it became clear by the look on Moses's face that Jackson was of some concern to him. Jason wondered who else might be involved. He was still thinking that the old bag lady had something to do with it, but he was not sure what.

Just as it looked like Moses might talk, the door opened and a woman police officer walked in. Jason had not wanted to be disturbed, but to Moses it was a welcome break.

"Lieutenant, I'm sorry to disturb you, but Sergeant Walker just called in. He would like you to meet him where the body was found last night. He said it was very important."

"Thanks. Have one of the officers put Mr. Moses in a cell until I get back. Make sure it's a private cell. I don't want him to have any contact with anyone, and I mean anyone. Do you understand?" he ordered.

"Yes, sir."

"I'll be back to talk to you in a little while. You think about what I said, Moses."

Jason got up and walked out. He drove over to the corner of Shields and Drake. It didn't take him long to find Sergeant Walker along with several men from the police lab looking through the area for evidence.

"What ya got?" he asked as he walked up to Jeff.

"Looks like a stash. Look," Jeff said.

Jeff lifted up a trashcan. Under the trashcan was a board. When Jeff lifted up the board, there was a small metal box.

"How did you ever find that?"

"I accidentally knocked the board to one side while we were going through the trash can looking for evidence. You said to go over the place with a fine tooth comb," Jeff said with a grin.

"What's in the box?"

"We haven't moved it yet."

"Go ahead, you found it."

Jeff was already wearing rubber gloves, so he bent down and lifted the box out of the hole. Using his pocketknife, he opened the box. Inside, they found a plastic bag that contained almost two dozen-credit cards, two hundred dollars in cash, and a couple of diamond rings.

"What do you make of this?" Jeff said as he looked up at Jason.

"I think you're right. You found their stash."

"Why would anyone stash this stuff here?"

"It's probably close to whoever stole it," Jason said as he looked around.

"You mean that Jackson lives around here?"

"No. I think the old bag lady that found Kandace's purse and briefcase lives around here. I think she's the ringleader," Jason said as his thoughts suddenly started to come together.

"What about the bum we found killed here?"

"My guess is that Harry...."

"Who's Harry?" Jeff asked.

"Harry is the guy you've got on the slab in the morgue. I think he came to get his share of the take, and maybe a little extra, but got caught raiding the cookie jar."

"Do you think Jackson killed him?"

"Maybe, but I doubt it. Jackson's in hiding, but I'm not sure that he is hiding from us. I think he might be hiding from someone else."

"Who?"

"I know this is going to sound strange, but I think he is part of a gang that has been mugging people for their house or apartment keys, as well as their credit cards and cash."

"What did they get from Miss Clarke's apartment?"

"Nothing that I know of, but she didn't have very much. Being blind, she has books that are in Braille, and books on tapes. They never thought that she wouldn't have much use for a television or VCR, the two items that can be disposed of quickly. They did get her credit cards and what money she had."

"Do you think that is why they ransacked her place?" Jeff asked.

"Probably. When they found out there was little in her apartment that they could resell, they trashed it. When they found out that the police were on their trail so quickly, the leader got scared and didn't need that kind of attention. My best guess is she killed Harry when he wanted more so he could get lost for awhile."

"You said 'she'. You think the bag lady is the leader?"

"Yeah, I do," he said as he began to review in his head what had happened over the past few days.

By talking out loud, Jason had convinced himself that he was on the right track. But where was the track taking him? He had his theory, but no proof. Someone had to know where the old bag lady was, and who she was.

Jason took a minute to look around. From the location of the trash container, he could see a total of three apartment balconies. One was on the first floor and two were on the second floor of an apartment less than fifty yards from the trash container.

He studied the apartment building for a minute. If under the trash can was the hiding place, what better place to live than just a short distance away. It would make it easy to watch and easy to defend if someone found it. It also would make it easy to disappear, if necessary, as there were several roads in and out of the apartment complex.

"I want that apartment complex closed off right now. I want everyone going in and out checked," Jason ordered.

"What?"

"You heard me. You're looking for a woman that has a birthmark under her left eye. It looks like dirt, but it's a birthmark. The woman may look like she's in her forties, or she may look much older. Just watch for the birthmark."

"Yes, sir," Detective Walker answered.

Walker was a little surprised at Lieutenant Barrett's sudden set of orders, but he had worked with him long enough to know that he should never question them. He also knew from experience, that Lieutenant Barrett was right far more times than he was wrong.

"Jeff, get some men in that building. I want the three apartments that you can see from here checked first."

Jeff quickly gave the order, then turned back to Jason. "What are you thinking?"

"I've got a gut feeling that the woman we want lives in one of those three apartments."

"Any proof?"

"None. None at all. Just a gut feeling," Jason admitted. "If no one is in the apartment, then find out who lives there or who is renting them. I want names. Let me know what you find out. I'm going to pay our friend McDonnally a visit."

"Right."

"And Jeff, don't take any chances. I think she's killed before."

"Right," Jeff replied with a quick nod, then turned and started toward the apartment building.

Jason watched Jeff head off toward the apartments. Once he was out of sight, he instructed the lab men to bag all the stuff and check it for fingerprints and anything else that might help in the investigation. He then returned to his car and left for McDonnally's bar.

CHAPTER SEVENTEEN

Jason drove up in front of McDonnally's bar and shut off the engine. He took a couple of minutes to look at the building again. The small neighborhood bar was showing the wear of years of neglect. The place needed painting and the sidewalk was cracked and broken. The windows were dirty and the signs were old.

Jason got out of the car and walked into the bar. Once inside, he found the place to be deserted. There was no one in sight, not even McDonnally.

As Jason walked up to the bar, he noticed that the cash register drawer was open. He leaned over the bar in order to get a better look and to see if the drawer was empty. When he leaned over, he noticed a hand on the floor behind the bar.

Jason hurried around the end of the bar and discovered McDonnally lying on the floor. After checking to see if he was still alive, he called 911 and asked that an ambulance be dispatched to the bar immediately.

McDonnally was alive, but not by much. He had a pulse, but it was weak and irregular. He was also unconscious.

Jason grabbed a bar towel and applied pressure to the wound in McDonnally's chest. He was not sure that McDonnally would survive until the ambulance arrived.

By the time the ambulance arrived, McDonnally was dead. After he was taken away, Jason took time to look around the bar. It was then that he remembered that he had put the place under twenty-four-hour surveillance. Where were the officers assigned to watch the bar, he wondered?

Just then he heard someone coming into the bar. He turned around to see Officers Wallace and Morris come in.

"Where the hell have you two been?"

"What do you mean," Morris asked. "We just got here."

"I ordered this place to be watched twenty-four hours a day."

"Our orders were to watch for Jackson. If he came around, we were to follow him and arrest him away from the bar."

"Did you see Jackson?"

"Yes, but we lost him about three blocks from here. We came right back and saw your car out front."

"Was Jackson in the bar?"

"Yeah. He came in, then left a few minutes later. We tailed him to a boarding house. By the time we found out what room he was in, he had gone out the back. You couldn't have missed him by very much. We haven't been gone more than fifteen, twenty minutes at the most," Wallace explained.

"Well, he was here long enough to kill McDonnally," Jason said, frustrated with how things were turning out. "Did you see anyone else come in the bar?"

"Yeah. We saw a woman. She was about five foot four inches tall, maybe five-five. About a hundred and thirty to a hundred and forty pounds, and curly brown hair. She was wearing a black coat, dark slacks, and no hat. I would say the woman was in her late forties or very early fifties."

"Yeah, that's about right," Morris added.

"Did she have a spot on her face, a spot that looked like it might be dirt under her left eye?"

"I didn't notice," Morris answered, then looked toward Wallace.

"I didn't notice, either. She was kind of far away to notice something like that."

"Okay," Jason replied.

Now he had two suspects, Jackson and the woman. It was clear that Jackson could have killed McDonnally and Harry, but it was also clear that the woman could have done it, too. The more he thought about it, the more convinced he became that the woman did it. He had no evidence to support his belief, but he was sure he would find it, sooner or later.

"You guys wait here until the lab boys get here. I want this place gone over from top to bottom."

"Yes, sir," Morris replied.

Jason left the bar and returned to his car. He sat in it for a few minutes as he thought about what was going on. It had been years since he had worked on a case that seemed to be so mixed up. There had to be something out there that would bring it together, a piece of evidence, a witness, something. Someone had to know something about the woman.

The more he thought about it, the more he felt that the one person who could put it all together was the old bag lady. There had to be a common thread between the old bag lady and the woman who had used Kandace's credit card.

Just as he was about to drive off, a call came over his police radio.

"Dispatch, Four Adam twenty-seven."

"This is Four Adam twenty-seven."

"Lieutenant Barrett, I got a call from Detective Walker. He wants you to meet him at the apartment complex. He said you would know which one."

"I know. Thanks."

He dropped the mike on the seat, then shifted the car into gear. After making a U turn in the middle of the street, he drove directly to the apartment complex near where Harry's body had been found. He found Detective Walker waiting for him in front of the apartment building that overlooked the drainage ditch.

"What's up," he said as he got out of his car.

"Apartment 2C is currently rented to a Miss Julie Baker. The manager described the woman as about five foot four or five, reddish brown hair, a little on the heavy side but not too bad, and in her mid-to-late forties."

"Sounds a little bit like our woman in the bar except for the color of her hair."

"She could be wearing a wig," Walker suggested.

"Probably. The height, weight and age are pretty close."

"The manager said that he saw her yesterday, but he hasn't seen her around today."

"What about the other apartments," Jason asked.

"One is vacant, the other is rented to a college professor in his early sixties."

"Ask the manager if he would show us the empty apartment."

"Right," Walker said then turned and started for the manager's office.

Within a few minutes, Walker returned with a passkey to the empty apartment. Jason followed Walker down the hall. When they arrived at the empty apartment, Walker slipped the key into the door and opened it.

Walker walked into the room, followed by Jason. Jason went directly to the balcony and looked out toward the drainage ditch. He could easily see the trash container where they had found the loot. A quick look around revealed that the apartment next door and the one above would have just as clear a view of the trash container.

Jason turned around. He stood quietly as he took in the room. He wanted a good idea what to expect when he got a warrant to search the apartment next door.

"Walker?"

"Yeah," he answered as he came out of the bedroom.

"Is the apartment that's rented to this Miss Julie Baker the same as this one?"

"According to the manager, it is."

"I want a man in this room twenty-four hours a day. I want Miss Baker arrested if she shows up at her apartment. Be sure you tell him not to take any chances. I believe she has killed before. I got a feeling that she won't be back, but I don't have anything else going for me right now."

"Okay," Jeff agreed.

"Get the rest of the officers out of the area. I want her to think that we've gone other places. I don't want to scare her off."

"Right."

Jason left the apartment and went to his car. He got in and started back toward the police station. He still had Moses on ice. It was time to find out what he knew.

Jason looked at his watch. It was a little past lunchtime. He wondered if Kandace had gotten something for lunch. He thought for a minute, then decided he would stop by and check on her before going to talk to Moses, just in case she hadn't had lunch.

* * * *

Lunchtime had come and gone, and Jason did not show up to take Kandace to lunch. She was disappointed, but she knew that Jason had things to do.

"Marsha, would you mind taking me to the lunchroom? I don't think Jason is going to be able to make it, today."

"Not at all."

Kandace stood up and waited for Marsha. Marsha took Kandace's hand and placed it on her arm, then started for the lunchroom.

"You need to tell me about this handsome man you're spending so much time with," Marsha said as she led Kandace out into the hall.

"There's really nothing to tell."

"Come on. This is Marsha you're talking to. We've been working together too long for you to pull that on me. Besides, I saw how you two were at the ice cream parlor. Now tell me, what's he like?"

"He is handsome," Kandace said with a shy giggle.

She felt like a schoolgirl talking to her best friend about one of the boys she liked.

"You can say that again. Is he really a cop?"

"Oh, yes. He is Lieutenant Detective Jason Barrett," she declared proudly.

"How did you two meet?"

"On the street, literally. He found me after I was attacked. He held me in his arms while we waited for the ambulance to arrive."

"How romantic. Kind of your own personal knight in shining armor. There to protect you from the evil dragon."

"Well, not exactly. It's more of a case of protecting me so I can identify the men who attacked me. I'm the only lead they have at the moment."

"You're kidding."

"No," she replied softly.

"Where are you staying? I tried to call you when I got back in town, but I didn't get an answer. I didn't even get your answering machine."

"I'm not staying in my apartment. I just couldn't stay there after it was broken into and torn apart."

"I didn't know about that."

Kandace's thoughts turned a little more serious with the mention of her apartment. She was dreading the move she knew she would have to make.

"Here we are. The chair is at your left hand."

"Thanks," Kandace said as she reached out and touched the back of the chair.

"I have a couple of things I have to do. Will you be all right until I get back?"

"Sure. The waitress knows me. She'll help me order."

"I'll be back in about forty-five minutes. You're going to have to tell me more about this lieutenant of yours."

"Okay."

Kandace could hear the sound of Marsha's footsteps as she left the lunchroom.

"Hi, Miss Clarke. Its' me, Sue."

"Hi, Sue."

"What can I get for you today?"

"How about a tuna sandwich on toast and a glass of milk."

"With or without chips?"

"Without, please."

"Coming right up," Sue said, then hurried off to the kitchen.

Kandace thought about Sue for a second. She was very typical of those who weren't sure of themselves around blind people. She wanted to be as much help as possible, but didn't know how.

She remembered the first time she was there. Sue asked Marsha what Kandace would like for lunch instead of asking Kandace directly. Over the past year that Sue had worked in the lunchroom, she had become much more relaxed around Kandace, and had become a help to her.

"Here you go, Miss Clarke," Sue said as she set the plate on the table. "Sandwich, dead ahead, your milk at two o'clock."

"Thanks, Sue."

"You're welcome," Sue said, then returned to the counter.

Kandace began to eat her sandwich. As she did, her thoughts turned to Jason. She wondered if he was getting anything to eat. She also thought about the questions that Marsha had asked her. She wondered why she didn't just come right out and tell her that she was staying at Jason's apartment instead of avoiding the question.

Marsha was her only friend there. She had often encouraged Kandace to go out with men, not to shut herself off from the rest of the world just because she was blind. Marsha was the one person that she felt she could talk to. She resolved to tell Marsha about her romantic interest in Jason as soon as she came back, but she would keep the more intimate moments with Jason to herself, at least for now.

The thought of her intimate moments with Jason caused her to remember how it felt to be held in his arms. She also thought about how good it felt to be touched by him.

Then her thoughts turned to something much more serious to her. She had spent the night with him because she loved him. But her statement to Marsha reminded her of the reason they were thrown together in the first place. It once again caused her to question their relationship, and the foundation it was built upon.

Was Jason really just protecting her because she was the only witness to a rash of crimes, or did he really love her as he had said? Had she read more into his apparent concern for her than he had intended? What would happen to them when the case was solved? Would he still want to see her, or would he simply disappear from her life?

But as her thoughts turned to how he held her, and how he made love to her, she could not believe her own doubts about his feelings for her. Yet, no matter how hard she tried, she could not completely dispel her doubts, either. She had been hurt once before when a boyfriend found that he could not cope with her blindness. She knew that she was setting herself up for a lot of pain if it turned out that Jason could not deal with it, either.

Kandace's thoughts were a little depressing to her. She loved him and had given herself to him. She wanted so much for things to work out for them. She wanted nothing more than to have him love her.

"Excuse me, but are you Miss Kandace Clarke?"

The voice was that of a woman. It was a soft voice, almost a whisper. It was also an unfamiliar voice.

"Yes," she answered cautiously. "Who are you?"

"I'm Officer Mary Bolman. I was asked to come and get you."

Kandace's heart sank. If anyone came for her from the police department, she was sure that it meant that something had happened to Jason.

"Is Jason, Lieutenant Barrett, all right?"

"He's just fine. He asked me to come and get you. It seems they have arrested a man, and he wants you to see if you can identify him."

"Oh, I see."

Kandace felt a little relieved that Jason was not hurt, but disappointed that he had not come to get her himself. She stood up and reached out a hand. The woman took hold of her hand.

"Please, let me hold onto you. It is easier for me," Kandace said.

It was clear to Kandace that the policewoman had never led a blind person around before.

"Okay," the woman agreed.

Kandace took the woman's arm and allowed the woman to lead her out of the lunchroom and into the hall. As they walked toward the elevator, Kandace thought she could hear someone close behind, someone in sneakers or some other kind of soft-soled shoe. When they stopped to wait for the elevator, she was sure that whoever was behind them had also stopped. She could sense that whoever it was, he was standing very close to her.

She heard the elevator door open and the woman guided her in. She heard the footsteps of the person behind her follow her into the elevator.

As the elevator door closed, Kandace turned around. The elevator started to move. She could smell an odor that seemed familiar to her. It was something that she had not smelled in that building before, but something that she smelled some place else.

Suddenly, she remembered where she had smelled it before. It was the smell of the man who had attacked her. It was that musty smell of his old coat that had been sweat in. Her mind was trying to think of what she should do. She thought about telling the policewoman, but it might endanger her if she told her now.

It was then that the thought crossed her mind that the woman might not be a police officer. If that was the case, she was being kidnapped. She was not sure what to do, but she could not just let them take her in broad daylight. She had to do something.

Kandace moved forward slightly as if adjusting her position. With her free hand, she reached out and touched the elevator door. The building was not a real busy place, but there was almost always people milling around in the main floor lobby. Someone would be in the lobby. Someone would certainly help her if she made a big enough commotion.

Kandace felt the elevator slow, then come to a stop. She could feel the door open as it slid by her fingers. When the door was open, she let go of the woman's arm and charged forward. She had no idea what or who she might run into. By taking the chance that there would be enough people in the lobby to cause a commotion, maybe it would be enough to make her abductors run off and leave her alone.

* * * *

Jason was standing in front of the elevator waiting for it to open. He was looking at the floor, but he was not really seeing it. He was deep in thought.

His thoughts were distracted by the ding of the elevator bell. As he looked up, the door opened. Before he could even say her name, Kandace came charging out of the elevator and ran right into him.

In an effort to protect her as well as himself, Jason wrapped his arms around as they went over backwards, crashing to the floor.

Everything happened so fast that Jason did not have time to react. As he was falling, he realized that something was wrong, but he didn't know what.

"Help me," Kandace yelled, still not aware that she was in Jason's arms.

"It's me, Jason."

"It's him, it's him," she cried out.

Jason rolled her off him and looked up in time to see the woman and Jackson running out of the building. As he scrambled to his feet he saw Marsha coming toward him.

"Take care of her," he called out to Marsha, then took off toward the door at a run.

Jason knew that it would be hard to catch them as they had a good lead on him. When he got to the street, he stopped and looked down the street. They were gone.

"Damn," he said under his breath.

"You looking for the woman and man who just came running out of that building."

Jason swung around to find a tall gray-haired man looking at him.

"Yeah. Which way did they go?"

"You won't ever catch them."

"Thanks for the advice, but which way did they go," Jason asked angrily as he looked around to see if he could figure out which way they went.

"Don't waste your time chasing them. I know where they're going."

Jason turned and looked at the man with surprise. He wasn't sure if he should believe him or not, but what choice did he have now. By now they could be anywhere.

"Do you know them?"

"I sure do. The man is Jackson, Carl Jackson. And the woman is the meanest woman on the streets."

"What's her name?"

"She's known on the street as 'Scissor Annie', but her real name is Ann Blank."

"How do you know that?" Jason asked, suspicious of the man.

"I'm one of the survivors, one of the few survivors."

"I don't understand, you're going to have to explain that to me."

"Scissors Annie carries a pair of scissors that are long and sharp as a razor, and she won't hesitate to use them on you. I saw her stab a guy with those scissors just because she didn't like the way he looked at her shopping cart," the man said.

Jason watched the man as he opened his coat and pulled his shirt out of his pants. On his stomach was a long thin scar.

"That's where she got me. She left me for dead, but it was freezing out that night. I was lucky. I was found before I bled to death."

"How would you like to get even for that?" Jason asked as the man tucked his shirt in.

"I sure would. What do I have to do?"

"Why don't you wait over there at the cafe," Jason said as he gave the man a ten-dollar bill. "I'll be back in a little while. When I get back, we'll talk about this 'Scissor Annie'."

The man looked at the ten-dollar bill, then up at Jason. After a moment or two of hesitation, he took the bill and smiled at Jason.

"See you in a little while," the man replied, then turned and started off across the street.

Jason watched him go across the street. Something about the man convinced Jason that he knew a lot about 'Scissor Annie'. He talked like he was well educated and well informed, even though his clothes indicated otherwise.

Jason watched the man go into the cafe, then turned around and went back into the building to see if Kandace was okay.

CHAPTER EIGHTEEN

Jason returned to the lobby to find that Kandace was not there. Figuring that Marsha must have taken Kandace back to her office, he hurried up the stairs to the second floor. When he went into the office, he found Kandace sitting on a sofa. She had her hands over her face. She was shaking uncontrollably.

Marsha was sitting beside her, holding her in her arms and trying to comfort her. She looked up at Jason, her eyes begging him to help her.

Jason walked over to the sofa. Marsha let go of Kandace and moved out of the way. Jason sat down and took Kandace in his arms.

"It's okay," he whispered.

"They were going to kidnap me. The one that hurt Chester was here. He was here, here in the building," she cried, her voice trembling.

"I know," he replied calmly as he guided her head to his shoulder.

"He was here in the building," she cried.

"I know. He won't ever get that close to you again," Jason promised.

Marsha stood near the desk. She felt helpless to help her friend. But as she watched Jason comforting Kandace, she realized that he could do more to settle her shattered nerves than she could ever do. It was not hard for Marsha to see that Jason was more than just a cop to Kandace, more than just her protector. It was clear that Kandace had fallen in love with him.

It was also clear to Marsha that Kandace meant more to Jason than just someone he was charged with protecting. He appeared to be truly concerned about her. The worried look on his face was that of someone with deep feelings for her, someone who really cared about her.

"I think I'd better go. It looks like you have things well in hand. You take good care of her," Marsha said as she moved toward the door.

Jason watched Marsha walk out of the office and close the door behind her. He thought for a moment about Marsha's last comment. He suddenly felt that he was not taking very good care of her if someone like Jackson and Blank could walk into her office so easily. He would not let that happen again.

He reached down and took Kandace's chin in his fingers. He lifted her face up and looked at her. Tears had streaked her face. He reached up and wiped the tears from her cheeks.

"It's all right," he reassured her. "I won't let them get near you again."

Kandace reached up and put her fingers on his face. Feeling the lines on his face, she could tell that he was afraid for her. She lightly slid her fingers to the sides of his face, then leaned toward him until her lips touched his. When their lips touched, she slid her hands around behind his neck and pressed her lips harder to his.

Jason wrapped her in his arms and returned her kiss with the same passion and love that she had given it. Holding her and kissing her made everything all right again for both of them.

When the kiss was over, Kandace laid her head back on his shoulder. She could hear his heart beat and hear him breathe. He was alive and that was enough.

"Honey, I'm going to have to go," he said in a whisper.

"Please don't go," she pleaded.

"I have to."

"Do you really have to go right now?" she asked, knowing full well that he did.

"Yes. I've got a good lead as to where those two are hiding. I think they will return there to hide out for the rest of the day, then try to leave town tonight after dark."

"What makes you think they will wait until after dark? Why won't they leave now?"

"They have been seen by someone who can identify them on sight. There is less chance of them being seen at night. You also have to remember they usually work after dark. They feel less apt to get caught at night," he explained.

"Yes, of course," she replied feeling a little stupid for not thinking of that herself.

"I'll have Officer Morris and Wallace take you to my place and stay with you until I get there. I'll have Marsha stay with you until they get here."

"Okay," she replied reluctantly.

Kandace had agreed to wait for the officers, but Jason could tell that she was nervous about it. He couldn't blame her, after all, the last one to come and get her posed as a policewoman.

Jason let go of Kandace and went to the phone. He called dispatch and requested that Officers Morris and Wallace come to Kandace's office. He explained what they were to do.

He had Kandace page Marsha to come to her office. Once Marsha came in, Jason said goodbye to Kandace and kissed her on the forehead.

"Don't let anyone in this room except for Officers Morris and Wallace, do you understand?"

"Yes, and you take care of yourself. Kandace is in love with you," Marsha said in a whisper.

Jason looked at her for a second, than nodded that he knew Kandace loved him. After a quick glance back at Kandace, Jason left the office.

* * * *

When Jason entered the cafe across the street from the office building, he found the tall man enjoying a sizable lunch. Jason slid into the booth across from him.

"I'm Lieutenant Barrett of the Fort Collins Police Department. Where do we find Jackson and this 'Scissor Annie'?"

"You will find them in an old warehouse down by the railroad tracks near LaPorte Avenue. It's that old brick warehouse that has the dark colored shipping doors, and the green walk-in door on the north end."

"What makes you so sure they'll be there?"

"'Scissor Annie' is smart. She will know that you are looking for a middle-aged woman, about five-four and weighing about one hundred thirty to forty pounds, right?"

"Yeah."

"Well, she'll hold up there until things cool down around here, maybe three or four days. When she thinks that things have cooled down enough, she'll come out of that building looking like an old bag lady. With her makeup and extra clothes, she'll look like she's about five-three and a hundred and sixty to seventy pounds. She'll push that shopping cart of hers up and down alleys until she's sure she is not being followed."

"Then what?"

"Then she'll go to her garage, get her car and leave town."

"Where's her car?"

"It's in a storage garage on the east side of town."

Jason listened to what the man had to say. Although he was skeptical, the man seemed to know what he was talking about.

"What makes you so sure, she'll leave town?" Jason asked.

"It's getting too hot around here for her. She's killed too many people and she knows you're getting close.

"She came here from Des Moines. She left there because it got too hot for her there. She left Milwaukee for the same reason. It's her pattern," he explained.

"You seem to know a lot about her. How do you know all this?

"I've been tracking her for the past two years. It's taken me this long to get close to her."

"Who are you?"

"Let's just say that I'm one of her victims, one of the few who survived."

"Let's not," Jason said as a thought came to him. "Let's say you're a cop, probably from Milwaukee. I'm going to ask you one more time, who are you?"

He hesitated to answer. If Jason arrested him and ran a make on him, it would not take him long to find out who he was. If Jason knew who he was, he might prevent him from his revenge. But was revenge what he really wanted? He had given up enough of his life to find this woman, and he found her. Now it was time to let those entrusted with such things do their job.

"I'm William Smith, Bill Smith. I'm originally from Milwaukee, and I am an ex-cop. They took me off the case when I ended up involved in it.

"How did you end up involved in the case?"

"You see, my wife and one of her friends were killed by 'Scissor Annie' when she attacked us after we had been to a play at the Art Center in Milwaukee. We were returning to our car in a parking structure when we were attacked. She murdered my wife, her friend, and almost murdered me. She stole our credit cards, our money, our car and the keys to our house. She went to our house and stole everything we had that was worth anything. I left the force to find 'Scissor Annie' when she left the Milwaukee area."

"I'm sorry," Jason said, then continued. "What gives with this woman? Why is it that she seems to have it in for people who are disabled?"

"She was raised by a mother who was in a wheelchair most her life. When she was a young girl all she heard from her mother was how depressed and terrible it was to be disabled. I guess something snapped in her head. After she was released from detention into the adult world, she began killing those people that were disabled and stole their valuables.

"Why would she attack you and your wife?

"You see my wife was in a wheelchair. She had been crippled in a car accident when she was a teenager."

"How did you find her?"

"The newspaper reports, mostly. They gave me the clues I needed to know that she had come here. I got here over three months ago and it has taken me all that time just to find her and where her hideout is located."

"Well, Mr. Smith, your hunt is over. I'll take it from here."

"I want to be there when you arrest her. I don't want her to get away again."

"She won't get away this time," Jason promised. "I have personal reasons for wanting her, too."

William looked into Jason's eyes. Something about the look on Jason's face told him that he would catch 'Scissor Annie' if anyone could.

"Okay, but be warned. She is deadly with those scissors of hers. She keeps them inside a slit in the right hand side of her coat, and she can get them out very quickly. They are long, thin and very sharp."

"Thanks for the warning. I'll remember that."

"I'll see you around. Thanks for the lunch."

"No problem. If you need anything, just give me a call at the police station."

"I will, Lieutenant. You be careful."

Jason watched as Smith slid out of the booth and stood up. He gave a nod to Smith, then watched him leave the cafe.

Jason's thought about what Smith had told him. What possible reason would Smith have to lie to him, he wondered? He could easily run a check on him. He wondered what he would find.

The waitress interrupted his thoughts. She said something, but Jason didn't hear her.

"Pardon me?" he asked as he looked up at her.

"I asked you if you want something, sir?"

Jason looked at the table, then back at the waitress.

"Ah, no. No, thank you," he said, then slid out of the booth.

Jason went out to his car. He made a quick call in and asked to have William Smith's story checked out. He then called Detective Walker and asked him to meet him in the Safeway Supermarket parking lot. When Jason arrived at the parking lot, he parked his car and waited for Walker.

Walker arrived shortly after Jason. He parked beside Jason's car and rolled down the window.

"What's up?"

"We have a name for our killer. Her name is Ann Blank. A source tells me she's holed up in the old Porter building down by the tracks."

"That warehouse hasn't been used in years," Walker said.

"Yeah. That's why it makes such a good hiding place. Let's get a backup and go check it out, but use a telephone. I got a feeling that Blank just might be monitoring the regular police radios. It would help explain why we never can seem to find her and why she was always one step ahead of us. Make sure they don't discuss any of this on the radio."

"Right," Walker said. "I'll meet you back here."

Jason nodded, then watched as Walker drove off. With nothing to do but wait, Jason leaned back and rested his eyes. It was no time to think about anything but Ann Blank and Carl Jackson. He needed nothing to distract him. He couldn't help it as his thoughts turned to Smith, and he wondered if he would have had that kind of dedication if 'Scissor Annie' had killed Kandace. After giving it some thought, he was sure he would.

Within a few minutes, Walker returned with two officers in a marked patrol car. Jason picked up a pad from the seat, then got out of his car and leaned against the trunk. Walker and the two uniformed officers joined him. Jason opened the pad as the others gathered around him. They listened and watched as Jason gave them instructions and diagrammed out his plan to capture 'Scissor Annie'. When the briefing was over, they all returned to their cars and drove to the old warehouse.

The uniformed officers covered the loading dock doors, while Walker and Jason went to the walk-in door. After giving everyone time to get into position, Jason banged on the door with his fist.

"This is the police. Come out with your hands up," Jason called out.

He waited, ready for anything. He had his gun in his hand, as did Detective Walker. There was no answer. Once again he banged on the door with his fist.

"We know you're in there. Come out, now."

Again there was no answer. Suddenly, they heard a crashing sound as if a window were breaking on the other the side of the building.

Jason stepped back away from the door. Walker looked at Jason for instruction. Jason motioned for him to check it out.

The air was suddenly filled with the sounds of gunshots. Jason turned and started to go to the corner of the building to see what was happening, but stopped. Something told him to hold his ground.

He heard something behind him. He turned around just as Ann Blank came charging out of the building with her scissors held firmly in her hand.

The gunshots had distracted Jason enough to put him off guard.

Ann Blank lunged at him with her scissors. Catching Jason off balance, she took a swipe at him. Jason tried to avoid the sharp scissors, but didn't quite make it. The sharp scissors penetrated through his coat and into his arm. Jason recoiled backward, tripping over a board and falling to the ground. As he fell, he dropped his gun.

Blank tried to take advantage of the situation and raised her hand up to stab at Jason again, but Jason was able to fend off the attack by kicking at her. He only managed to kick her in the arm as she swung the scissors at him, but it kept the scissors from sticking him again.

Realizing that he would have help any second, Blank turned and started running. Jason rolled over, picked up his gun and scrambled to his feet. His arm hurt like hell, but he could not let her get away. He aimed his gun at her and called to her.

"Halt," he yelled.

She stopped, turned around and looked at Jason. She stood still with her scissors in her hand. She could see that he had his gun pointed at her.

"Put your hands up," he ordered sharply.

Slowly, a smile came over her face as she looked at him. Suddenly, she looked toward the warehouse and saw Walker coming around the corner. She turned and started to run again.

"Halt, damn it," Jason cried out.

She didn't halt that time. Jason aimed carefully, then squeezed the trigger. There was a loud bang as his gun jumped in his hand. He saw Blank stop abruptly and reach a hand around to her back.

Slowly, she turned around and looked at him. Her eyes were big and her mouth was wide opened. She looked surprised that he had actually shot her.

Jason slowly moved toward her. He noticed that she still had the scissors in her hand.

"Drop the scissors," he ordered, then stopped.

She just looked at him for a second or two, then began staggering toward him. The closer she got, the higher she held the scissors. When she was only a few feet away from Jason, she stopped as if she was unable to move any closer.

"Drop the scissors," Jason ordered as he pointed his gun right at her face, but she just looked at him.

She began to sway back and forth a little, and then began to stumble. Still holding the scissors high above her head, she looked from Jason to Walker who was now standing next to Jason. Walker also had a gun pointed at her. She stood as if she were ready to strike out, but seemed confused, disoriented. Not sure what she should do with both of them ready to shoot.

"Drop the scissors," Jason demanded a third time.

"Never," she replied in a weak, yet defiant voice.

Suddenly, her knees buckled and she fell to the ground on her knees. She looked up at Jason. There was no fear or anger in her eyes any more. The look in her eyes showed a resignation to the fact that it was over. It was the end.

Suddenly, in one swift move, she put the point of the scissors to her stomach and pushed the point deep into herself.

She looked up at Jason and smiled. After a few seconds the smile faded and she toppled over. She lay dead on the ground just a few feet from him, dead by her own hand.

Jason just stood there looking at her. She had killed several people in the past few years, now she had killed herself. It seemed to Jason that justice had been served. Once again, people would be able to walk freely without fear from her. But Jason knew that it would be a long time before some of the folks around there would once again feel safe in old town.

"I'm glad that's over," Walker said.

"Yeah, me too," Jason replied.

Walker looked over at Jason. He noticed that there was blood on Jason's sleeve.

"Jason, you're bleeding."

Jason looked down at his arm. There was blood dripping off his fingertips and blood on the sleeve of his coat.

"I'll take you to the hospital," Walker said as he started to lead Jason to the car.

Jason stopped and looked back toward the building. He had not seen Jackson. He had no idea what had happened around back of the building where all the shooting had been.

"Where's Jackson?" Jason asked as he saw the uniformed officers coming around the corner of the building.

"He refused to give up and was shot when he tried to escape. He's dead, too," Walker said as he took Jason by the arm and once again started toward the car.

Walker drove Jason directly to the emergency room of the hospital while the other officers stayed on the scene. After Jason's wound was stitched up and his arm put in a sling, he returned to the police station for debriefing by the shooting team investigators. He knew there would be a hearing before a board. It happens every time an officer fires his gun, other than on the practice range. The hearing would come only after a complete investigation of the incident which would take a few days. Right now, it was time to go to Kandace.

Jason arrived home shortly after dark. It had turned cold and it felt as if it might snow tonight.

As he walked into the apartment building, he noticed the patrol car parked out front. He felt a little better knowing that Kandace had someone with her.

When Jason opened the door to his apartment, he found Officers Morris and Wallace in his living room. Officer Morris was standing near the bedroom door with his gun in his hand, while Officer Wallace was at the kitchen door. He also had his gun in his hand. The two officers put their guns away and relaxed as soon as they saw that it was Lieutenant Barrett.

"What happened to you?" Morris said when he noticed that Jason's arm was in a sling.

"I got stabbed while trying to make an arrest."

"You okay?" Wallace asked.

"Yeah. I'll be fine. Where is she?" Jason asked.

"In the bedroom. She went straight to the bedroom as soon as we got here. Pretty tough day for her," Wallace said, the tone of his voice showing that he understood how difficult the day had to have been for her.

"She gets around pretty well, doesn't she," Morris said.

"Yeah. Say, thanks for sticking around, but I can take it from here."

"Sure," Wallace replied, then turned toward the door.

Morris followed Wallace out of Jason's apartment, shutting the door on their way out. As soon as they were gone, Jason tossed his coat over the back of a chair, then went to the bedroom door. He knocked lightly on the door and waited for a response.

"Come in," Kandace said.

Jason opened the door. The light from the living room spread over the bed. Kandace was lying on top of the comforter, still in her street clothes.

"What is it?"

"It's me."

"Jason," she called out excitedly as she sat up. "Are you all right?"

"Yes, I'm fine. I didn't want to disturb you if you were sleeping, but I wanted you to know that I'm home."

"Come here."

Jason walked over to the bed and sat down on the edge. He reached out and put his hand on the side of her face.

She reached out and touched his arm. Almost immediately she realized that something was wrong. She lightly ran her hand over the sling on his arm.

"You've been hurt!"

"Just a scratch."

"They don't put your arm in a sling for just a scratch," she said, the tone of her voice demanding answers.

"Well, maybe it's a little more than a scratch. The woman that tried to kidnap you stabbed me with a pair of scissors."

Jason saw the worried look on her face. It was strange, but he actually liked the fact that she was truly worried about him.

"I'll be fine in a week or so. Nothing serious. If it will make you feel any better, I'll let you take care of me for awhile," he said as he lightly touched her cheek.

"I love you," she whispered. "I would like to take care of you."

"How would you like to take care of me for a very long time?" he asked as he lightly touched her cheek with his hand.

Kandace looked toward him. She could hardly believe what she heard. She had thought about it, but had not expected him to just blurt it out like that.

"I don't know," she replied.

"I understand. It's kind of sudden," Jason said, wishing he had waited for a more appropriate time.

"I don't know if your landlady will allow a Seeing Eye Dog in her apartment building," Kandace said with a smile.

"She better, or we'll have to find another place to live."

Kandace reached out to Jason. He leaned over her and kissed her. It was a long passionate kiss, the kind meant to say, "I'll love you forever."